Paul Katsitis

Mikonos Crime 3
The Prince

Paul Katsitis

Mikonos Crime three

The prince

Original Title in German/Greek: "Khaled"

So far in this series appeared:

Mikonos Crime 1 Abducted
Mikonos Crime 2 Confusion
Mikonos Crime 3 The Prince
Mikonos Crime 4 Spy (Feb 20)

Published in German and Greek:
Mykonos Crime 1 Die Bestie von Mykonos
Mykonos Crime 2 Rache
Mykonos Crime 4 Der Drei-Sterne-Mord
Mykonos Crime 5 Tattoo
Mykonos Crime 6 Skalpell
Mykonos Crime 7 Hass
Mykonos Crime 8 Sturm über Mykonos
Mykonos Crime 9 Die Maske
Mykonos Crime 10 Abseits
Mykonos Crime 11 Glut
Mykonos Crime 12 Putsch
Mykonos Crime 13 Royals
Mykonos Crime 14 Traumata
Mykonos Crime 15 Khaled
Mykonos Crime 16 Spione (Feb 20)

English and German/Greek volumes have
different numbers!

imprint
Cover picture: Gest. Katsitis / Porträtauf.
Shutterstock/istockphoto
Copyright Paul Katsitis 2019
Production and Publishing:
BoD- Books on Demand, Norderstedt

ISBN 9783750429727

Unfortunately, many gay books remain unpublished because translation costs are high, and publishing is therefore unprofitable. So, I asked a Greek friend who was born in London to translate the series. He is not a professional translator.

So, come across mistakes: smile and read on. And remember: His English is certainly better than your Greek :)

Thanks, Antonis!

Each volume deals with a completed case, so the volumes do not need to be read in order.

All the books of the series were set in Greece. Since Greek typesetters cannot detect any mistakes in English, there are certainly more mistakes in the book than in a normal book. But so at least a few euros remain in Greece.

Angelos Nikakis, 30, was chief commissioner in Thessaloniki. During a vacation in Mikonos he met

Alexandros Nikakis (formerly Galis), 36, the chief commissioner on Mikonos. One week after getting to know each other, they got married.
A year later, Angelos Nikakis was elected mayor. The first gay mayor in Greece.

Everything went perfect – until …

Khaled Al-Massawi, 25, arrived for a short break on Mikonos. Khaled is crown prince of a small Emirate and fell madly in love with Angelos, who suddenly did not know anymore to whom he belongs.

In "Abducted" the Emirate was called Sharjah. Due to legal reasons this had to be changed.

1

Thessaloniki

Adam Resniak lay on the floor of his living room in the small studio apartment in Thessaloniki. He was in pain and almost could not move because he could barely breathe.
The bullet had hit the left side of the chest, which always led to a certain unpleasant shortness of breath. Adam rolled onto his right side and the pain subsided.
Two minutes longer, it will not take longer, he thought. Patience was part of his job. Sometimes he had to wait for hours, without moving. Nevertheless, he must not lose to pay attention. Because within fractions of a second he had to react. And push off.
Despite the pain he had to smile inside. It was a joke. Me, one of the most demanded professional killers in Europe, catch a bullet for myself. In addition, in my own apartment. The colleague must have fired from the opposite roof. Slowly, the pain improved, but Adam Resniak decided to stay a little longer on the

ground. Although the colleague should have immediately disappeared right after the precision shot: only a great deal of caution had let him survive so long. Carpe Diem. Use the time. Who could be the client? Still lying, he went through the list of the last "customers", but also the "target objects". Well, none of the latter was alive, for Resniak knew his onions. Only in the last case he failed. He had sent a visitor to the afterlife instead of the target person. Looking through the sight pipe, Resniak had been sure the man was the target. Why did this jerk, who looked so much like the potential victim, had the idea to do a visit?

It was his last visit.

And Resniak had warned the real target person with his missed shot. He had then gone underground and, despite his almost unlimited resources, Resniak had failed to iron out his mistake.

The client was of course not pleased. Sure, Resniak had paid back the fee, but that was not the point.

A failure was unforgivable. And it was bad for the business, because the world of top professional killers was small, and the competitors were happy about everyone who bungled.

As a rule, one did not live long after a failed mission.

And that's why I'm lying here, Resniak thought.

But he smiled, began to roll to the right and sat up. After another minute, he got up and went to the bathroom.

He took off his sweater and examined the bullet-proof vest.

There was the stupid thing.

'Passable shot, colleague', Resniak thought.

Then he carefully removed the bullet-proof vest. There it was. The famous bruise that would hurt for a long time.

Although the west prevented the impact of the projectile, but not the hit and so you inevitably land by the force on the ground.

Adam Resniak knew his business. He knew that there was at least the possibility that an undelivered performance leads to a bullet. So, he had taken extensive security measures and decided not to go one step more without a vest. He knew that colleagues like to choose the chest as a target because you can do the greatest possible damage even in the absence of precision. Instead of the heart one often hits the liver: the result was the same, the death came only twenty minutes later. Or you hit the lungs, also mostly deadly. Resniak on the other hand preferred clean headshots, because he was an outstanding shooter. A burst skull is a very good sign for the death of the object. He rubbed the growing bruise with an ointment. He broke off the breathing exercises he regularly did to get a calmer hand.

Do not get impatient. You have just been shot.

Thankfully, the colleague had not chosen the lately popular method and set a booby trap. You open the door and you have a business ticket to the afterlife. However, the danger of being discovered is great. Not when triggering the explosion, but when laying the explosive trap.

But I would have recognized it in time, thanks to the scanner, which detects explosive charges from the outside and is also used at airports.

Being up to date with the latest technical standards is - as in other professions - important.

A training course for professional killers. Adam had to laugh about the idea. A bomb in this classroom would make the world suddenly safer.

Good. Thoroughly analyze the situation and draw the right conclusions. That has priority. His non-demise would become known after a few days. Still believed the colleague and thus his client, that Adam was history. But: this "protection by death" would not last for a long time.

I must be gone by then, Adam thought. He decided to mute himself and leave the house over the roof. Roofs had become his second home because they were the perfect location for his work. And offered numerous escape possibilities. A courageous jump over a street canyon, no problem for Adam. For his 43 years, he was extremely fit.

He had rented his apartment, partly because of the perfect escape conditions.

Two fire ladders and on two sides a jump to the neighboring house was possible. So, it was no problem to overcome two street canyons and land on a house in the parallel street. Resniak left the five-story building and walked at a normal pace towards the main train station. Fortunately, a strong wind blew and so his thick jacket and scarf did not attract attention. Salonika was not Athens.

He entered the concourse and turned right to the lockers. There still were lockers in the harbor terminal. In other cities they had already been removed due to possible bombings. Adam opened the compartment and pulled out a bag. He looked in for a moment. Everything is still there. Large sums in euros and dollars, small bags of diamonds and several passports. That would be enough to leave no trace. No credit card use, no cell phone call - avoid everything that would tell someone where you are. And nowadays you almost inevitably leave traces. Everything was better in the good old times. For professional killers, this usually stupid sentence was completely true.

Adam Resniak ran to the harbor. A fair distance, but taxis sometimes have cameras and dash-cams. A no-go. Admittedly, Adam had the ability to make himself almost invisible by ordinariness.

But beware ... well, we already talked about that. He stopped briefly and opened the bag in a side street. He was not sure if he put one or two Glocks into the bag. There were two. How gratifying. And his precision rifle, dissected clean. Of course, every escape which would lead to a check of his hand luggage was forbidden.

The official's face looking at the X-ray machine Resniak would have liked to see. Nearly a million in cash, two handguns and a rifle, diamonds and passports. No typical hand luggage.

Adam went to the counter of "Seajet" and looked at the electronic scoreboard. Stay domestic, to guarantee to leave no traces. But then the question arose whether he should choose a secluded location or rather a place where bustle prevails.

Samos. Too dead. Lesbos. Close to the Turkish border and therefore perfect for an escape. But ugly.

Resniak had a certain claim attitude. No luxury - that would be too dangerous in his profession. But it should not be too down-to-earth. In addition, Lesbos was full of refugees, which meant increased police presence, media ... No, I need an island with many people and as little police as possible. Santorini or Mikonos.

Santorini is too cheesy for me and there are too many Chinese and Resniak could not stand them.
Welcome to Mikonos, Adam said softly. We will get along well.
At 7.30 pm he entered the ferry towards Mikonos. The night ferry, arrival 10.30. Even if any police officer were on the scene, they would be mentally already in the end-of-work modus. I have to be gone by then, Adam thought.

2

Delos

Antonis Kyriakos looked outside. Despite the stained-glass windows of the chapel, he could clearly see the bustle on the waterfront of Mykonos. Crowds. Surprisingly, he heard nothing of it. It was quiet in the church, though it would not have surprised him if an ice cream-eating Chinese would pose in front of the icons to post something new on his Instagram account.

But Europeans and Americans are not better. No respect for anything. Especially not here on Mikonos. Yes - they come for party, shopping and drugs. Only a few people visit Delos, for Antonis the world's most unique place. An entire universe of antiquity - uninhabited for centuries and therefore protected from the "blessings" of the modern world. Only a small number, a very small number, visit the archeological park with its temples, the theater and the 3000-year-old stadium. The last remnant of those interested in culture in a world full of nothing and superficialities.

He could have included himself in his caustic criticism, but Antonis was not capable of so much self-criticism. He had already moved miles away from the former Antonis, who was studying archeology with much enthusiasm.

He studied in Thessaloniki, dreaming of being allowed to work on Delos. To discover something significant. His photo in a journal. The dreams of every student of wealth and professional success - still unencumbered by the realities and strokes of the life of a real adult.

What did Antonis do in the chapel? He lit one of the thin candles and put it in the wooden block.

He asked for forgiveness. Like most people, he did not go to church before doing something - HE could have contradicted or warned. No, first you do mischief and then you need a discharge certificate. And then continue subsequently without guilty conscience. In fact, Antonis felt much better after pausing in the chapel. He made his way through the masses, which pushed through the city before ten o'clock.

A cruise-ship-day. Plural.

Hate day for Antonis. These floating cities with their heavy-oil motors and the smoke-swans whose destructive power could be seen on Delos. Over the entire plant you could see the fine gray soot, which, paired with rain, overlays the sculptures like an acid. 3000 years had not affected them. And we can do it in 30 years with a few muddlers to destroy an ancient world.

Of course, it was not just the ships and by the way Antonis drove a brand-new SUV.

But man tends to make moral claims only to others, but to allow himself a certain Laisser-faire.

With divine relief Antonis entered the boat in the direction of Delos. Today it was only half filled - to his relief.

After only a few minutes he reached the island. Antonis passed the few people waiting in front of the entrance and waved to Lara, who was sitting at the cash point. At the sight of the statues and ruins Antonis got a bad conscience and for the tenth time he told himself that he could not continue like this. But the blame carry others. The ones who paid him and his colleagues so miserably that they all had to live in tiny rooms in the hinterland of Mikonos - or even here in the museum. Antonis avoided his colleagues. He was not in the mood for chatter. In addition, he was bothered by the heat that has been lying over the Cyclades for days so that no one had a dry shirt after 10.00 am. Sweating like in a sauna.

Delos is a single burning glass. No shade and the rock absorb the heat, so from noon on you could only work with gloves. Being an archeologist usually means heat and thirst. Respect for the colleagues in

Egypt, Syria and Iraq. They really give everything physically.

Antonis cursed. Delos, Mikonos and Renia. Here you can sweat to death at 2:00 pm, but at 2:30 pm you capture a lethal pneumonia when suddenly the cold north wind emerges. You have the choice between swimming trunks and autumn jacket.

Antonis sighed.

I am the black sheep. Certainly not the only one, but I do not honor my profession, Antonis thought.

He approached his current excavation area near the ancient theater. Almost 15,000 people once lived on the tiny island, which is just under 2 square kilometers in size. More populated than Hong Kong. Too tight, so that the construction of tombs was forbidden on Delos. Corpses had to be shipped to the neighboring island of Renia within six hours. Why the larger Mikonos was not populated was a mystery, especially as there was water on the large neighbor of Delos.

Today it is known that religious reasons attracted people to Delos. The birthplace of Apollo.

Antonis grabbed into his pocket to get his key, because the box of tools and paintbrushes always had to be locked. Too often, tourists took them away. What do they want with brushes and trowels, which are available in every home depot? It remains their secret. The only indication for Delos was his incised name, Kyriakos. Great souvenir. But with the locked boxes, this special souvenir shopping without credit card belongs to the past.

Antonis put the key in the lock. Why does the thing turn so easily? Antonis thought.

Then he saw a flash of lightning. In the last second of his life he still registered that his right arm flew away and was surprised that he felt no pain. He had already crossed the line between life and death.

3

Negev desert, Israel

Khaled al-Mussawi was out of his head most of the time. The crown prince of a small Emirate had lost all interest in the supposedly important issues of life. Politics, his hobbyhorse, and - after the death of his father - his future playing field: Khaled had lost all interest.

He had only one thing in his mind: Angelos.
Not only was Khaled in love, he had fallen for
another man.

They have met on Mikonos. Angelos Nikakis
was the commissioner and mayor of Celebrity
Island.

Khaled was paralyzed when Angelos smiled
at him for the first time. This man and no
other.

The problem was: Angelos was already
married to Alex. And happy, as Angelos
always emphasized. But Khaled noticed that
his open declaration of love was not flatly
rejected. Angelos began to doubt. Level 1.
Angelos was confused. Level 2. Angelos
realized that he loved Alex AND Khaled.
Level 3. Angelos said for the first time that he
loves Khaled. Level 4. One step - only one -
was still missing.

It was the best moment in Khaled's life.
Before, everything was dull and gray. Sure,
there is no lack of luxury. But the palace in
Fudscheirah was a prison and Khaled's father
the guard. And as if this wasn´t enough:
Khaled was gay. In Islamic countries a death
worthy "crime". He made his previous
experiences on trips abroad and always in
total secrecy, always trembling, he could be
discovered.

After that day on Mikonos, Khaled did not
care anymore

Angelos Nikakis would become the man of
my life. Angelos loves me as a human being.

Because luxury and the whole royal bric-a-brac does not interest him. An argument that was important to assess how serious Angelos' feelings were. Angelos had problems to call Khaled "your Royal Highness"! He always laughed. Wonderful.

Khaled was impressed. Normally, people always lay prostrate before him.

He thought back to the first night with Angelos and got goose bumps.

Khaled had never experienced such a body sensation. Or better: a waterfall of feelings.

It already crackles in the marriage of Angelos and Alex, Khaled knew that much. Angelos had told him that he would stay with Alex, but his eyes gave himself away. It was more gratitude and he was afraid of Alex' reaction to a possible separation.

That is not a sufficient basis. That cannot last for long, Khaled thought. From the beginning he had come up with a strategy: just wait until the last straw will break the camel's back.

Then the events would start rolling.

Khaled would tell his father that he must resign from the post of crown prince.

And confess - why admit? ... It's not a crime. No, he would tell him that he is gay. To prevent his father's stupid question about what he did wrong, Khaled would explain to him that this was a genetic predisposition. No, Father would not understand that either. And that Allah, God, or Yahweh created gay people, would transcend his father's horizon. The final blow will be when I tell him that I will soon marry a Greek mayor. The cardiac effects would be incalculable.

Khaled sighed as his advisors urged him to leave. The agents of the Israeli intelligence would become impatient. Months ago, Khaled would have been jubilant because his father chose him for this special mission. The common enemy Iran should lead to a new alliance between Israel and the Emirates. The talks should be conducted by the smallest of the Emirates to avoid any attention. If necessary, Dubai could speak of a solo run. A historic mission - I do not care anymore. I have only one mission: I MUST have HIM-
And I'll never give him up, if ...
Yes, if ...

4

In the house of the two commissioners Alexandros and Angelos Nikakis, there was a lot of tension in the air. Since Angelos felt in love with another man, nothing was the same as before.

Alex did not blame him directly. How can you accuse someone because of his feelings, even if it is your husband? Shit happens. And: Angelos was honest. He told Alex everything what happened and was obviously fighting against his feelings. In the end, Angelos decided to stay with Alex. Still, on some occasions Alex resented Angelos for having fallen in love with Khaled. Angelos´ fair offer to look for another place to stay had been rejected by Alex. Despite all, he did not want to lose his great love Angelos, but he did everything he could to spoil the mood. Silly comments like "It smells like sheikh here", were below the belt and beard witness to the psychological injuries.

Alex did not understand that he was pushing Angelos into Khaled's arms more and more. "We cannot continue like this", Angelos said angrily.

"Who keeps running after someone else? You're the one who wants something new. "

"I do not want anything. I have chosen you. But it does not seem to matter to you, the way you behave. "

"Am I cheating or you?"

"Khaled saved my life, also for you, remember?" Angelos growled. "And he had the wish to spend a night with me. I asked you if that's okay. Before. And you said 'yes'. And: I told Khaled it remains a one-time affair and that I love you. That he's a bloody Crown Prince and has money to burn has never played any role for me, if that's what you mean."

Alex sighed.

"No, I know that these things are rather repugnant to you. So, it seems that you love Khaled as a person. The bad thing is that I think he's a good guy."

"He IS a person with a good character, Alex. Just like you", Angelos said. "And I would stay with you if you would not have changed that way. Your taunts make my life hell! "

"I cannot tell you what's wrong with me. I cannot control it. I cannot live without you, but you do not have to stay just because of a feeling of obligation or gratitude. That would not be enough. It would not be enough for me - AND you "

"Maybe it's better for us both, if I will live somewhere else", Angelos replied.

"In the Emirates?", Alex asked.

"Definitely not. You forget that I'm the mayor. There is already enough gossip!"

"I know. The Emir of Mikonos and the Crown Prince of Fudscheirah, the dream couple par excellence", Alex replied.

"Cynicism does not suit you!"

'That was not cynical. The people of the island love you! "

And that was the truth. Angelos was among the sort of mayors who bend laws and ordinances until it creaks to get the best and most for his community. The fact that Angelos has a personal relationship with the Prime Minister certainly helped in some cases.

"I do not think they still love me when I leave you. People like you, too. Maybe I should resign", Angelos said dejectedly.

"Nonsense. There is no connection between one and the other."

"Some people will think different", Angelos said.

"But ok. It's probably best if I go! "

Alex was pale.

"No. I ... I cannot live without you. It's just not easy for me ... "

"Do you think for me? I'm going to the beach", Angelos said.

After Angelos arrived at the Kitesurfer´s Beach on the inner bay of Ornos, he picked up the phone. Calling is not possible, he thought. Who knows who is listening? An SMS is probably better.

MY PRINCE. THE CRISIS IS GETTING WORSE. AND I MISS YOU. ANGELOS.

It only took a few minutes for the answer to come:

HOW WOULD IT BE WITH A "I LOVE YOU,
KHALED ??"
Angelos smiled and tapped his cellphone:
"I LOVE YOU! BUT YOU ALREADY KNOW THAT! "

I have made one person happy today,
because Khaled loves me more than
anything on this world.
But before Khaled's answer arrived, the cell
phone growled.
"Emir, there is a dead man on Delos. A blast.,
We do not know yet, whether it was a
murder, or … " Giorgios said, Angelos' right-
hand-man in the town hall.
Angelos sighed.
"Giorgios, I hardly believe that there were gas
pipes in ancient Greece. What is going to
explode on Delos? And a terrorist attack on
an uninhabited island would also be
something unusual. Do you already know
who it is? "
"Uh, no. We do not have all the pieces
together! "
Oh, shoot, Angelos thought. The pathologist
will be happy.
"Already on the way", Angelos said.
I do not need to hurry because of a corpse
puzzle.

5

S witch off the Christmas lightning",
Angelos growled to Nikos and Tomas, the
two patrolmen, and he went to the
maritime police's boat.

"Yannis, let's go!"

"Aye, aye, Emir!"

I'll never get rid of that nickname, Angelos
thought. The trip by boat - of course with
flashing lights - took only a few minutes. At
the dock, Giorgios and Yannis
Papadopoulos, the director of the Delos
Archaeological Museum, were waiting.
The latter gesticulated wildly. Probably
because the island would be closed today,
and some entry fees would be lost. Angelos
saw how the last tourists left Delos. Under
protest, because the trip costs whopping 50
euros, which has upset Angelos for two years
and threatened the owner to block access to
the dock in the Old Harbor with grids. But the
owner was able to present a contract with
the community, which assured him the
exclusive rights for boat trips to Delos for the
next 50 years. Unfortunately, only 23 years
had passed yet.

"Where?", was the only word Angelos said.

"At the theater", Giorgios said.
The theater is located at the southern end of
the archaeological park, less than 300 meters
from the pier. In a field of ruins, an explosion

damage is difficult to detect. Lying stones and cubes abound. But Angelos knew "his" Delos, because the island not only belongs administratively to Mikonos, it is owned by the community.

The weather had changed, and the wind blew from constantly changing directions. According to legend, Aiolos, the god of the wind, lived on Mikonos. Why didn´t he chooses another island, Angelos growled, trying to dodge a cloud of dust - in vain. When translating to Delos, it had been almost windless. You did not see anything anymore and there was nothing on the island which offered any kind of protection. Forget about the forensics.

"I hope no finger flies into my face", Angelos said to Giorgios.

"Or the testicles. It was a male archaeologist who worked in the theater! "

"Thank you, Giorgios. That makes it easier", Angelos murmured between two clouds of dust.

"Where is the corpse? I hope in the visitor center ", Angelos roared against the wind. Giorgios nodded.

"The island stays closed until the wind subsides", Angelos yelled at Papadopoulos, who was on the rampage. But Angelos didn´t understand one word and simply grinned. It was not the first observation of a crime scene on Mykonos, which had to be postponed because of the weather.

Set up pavilions as in the TV crime story: an illusion. Angelos struggled trying to keep his balance.

The thermometer showed 24 degrees - it felt like 10. As a Greek from the mainland, he was still allergic to the gusty storms of the Aegean Sea.

Concentration ability zero. Alex always laughed when Angelos complained whiney about a storm.

"Stupid island. How can it be so windy in bright sunshine?"

"Don´t let your voters hear the 'stupid island'!" Alex was born on Mikonos and just shrugged his shoulders on days with Wind strength 8. "Soft breeze", was his usual comment.

When Angelos arrived inside the little museum, he took a deep breath first. Pure air without dust. Mikonos. Wrong world. Free breathing only inside, at least when Aiolos had a bad day.

"You got a coffee?", Angelos asked.

"I'm not ...", Papadopoulos began, but remembered that making the mayor angry is not in his own interest. And so, he runned along

"Finally. Where are the first, um, parts?"

Giorgios pointed to a corner where two policemen sorted with gloves or better: tried to sort.

'That's not a lot. The archaeologist is in worse shape than his ruins", Angelos whispered.

"Boss, that was a human being", Giorgios replied.

"You're right. Excuse me. I'm not myself today", Angelos said ruefully.

"The prince? Or Alex? "

"As if it could be separated", Angelos murmured.

"As I already told you, everybody in the town hall likes Alex ...". Angelos rolled his eyes.

"... but if you're happier with the prince, that's just how it is. We want a happy and satisfied boss. Then he is easier to handle!"

Angelos laughed.

He liked Giorgios very much. As a "right-man-hand" and because of its openness.

"Am I so obnoxious in the moment?"

"No. But depressed", Giorgios replied.

"It will change soon. I'll probably move soon! "

Giorgios looked at Angelos in horror.

"Permanently?"

Angelos shrugged.

"I'll undergo mental low-level flights the next few days. Keep an eye on me and tell me if I say or do something wrong! "

"Does the Emir love the prince?" Giorgios asked, adding humor to the conversation.

And indeed, Angelos had to laugh. He would never get rid of the nickname "Emir". The name had nothing to do with Khaled, rather with his rigid government style. But it was welcomed to the majority of the islanders, because finally things were tackled, which were laying undone for decades. More important, Angelos was not part of the island network. His only connection to Mikonos was originally only Alex.

"I love both. It's better in such a situation to step back ", Angelos said sadly.

Now Giorgios's face was filled with horror. Too loud he said:

"YOU CANNOT DO THIS TO US. AND NOT TO THE ISLAND!"

"Chill out. I have not decided yet, "Angelos replied.

"Whether Khaled or Alex. This is only a matter for you three. You are a good mayor. If you have doubts, call for a new election!"

Angelos thought for a moment.

'That would be an option. But honestly, I'm currently wondering where to stay!"

"Boss, you can always ..."

Angelos smiled.

'That is very kind. But my prince will find something. Probably overpriced! "

"As long as he pays, it's alright! Uh, how do we continue here?, Giorgios asked.

Angelos grinned.

"Do you see? I am so completely in disorder that I forgot the corpse. What does the weather forecast say for tomorrow?"

On Mikonos, two things are completely out of interest. Sunny or cloudy: it does not matter. The temperature: does not matter. Everything depends on one value: the wind strength and its direction. Everyone on the island knows - unlike mainlanders - the unit Bofors.

"Two to three. Gusts up to 35 ", Giorgios replied, after tapping for a few moments on his smartphone.

"And what do we have today?" Angelos asked.

"Four to five. Gusts up to 67 ", Giorgios replied.

"That is definitely true", Angelos snarled.

"Ok, Giorgios. Tomorrow everything stays closed here. And we meet at twelve! We do not inform the relatives yet!"

"Sorry, boss. But where can I find you if something extraordinary happens?"

Angelos shrugged again.

"If I would already know that. Uh, I will send you a text message! "

Papadopoulos came around the corner with a plastic cup. Definitely just black water, Angelos thought.

He was right.

6

The mood of Commissioner and Mayor Angelos Nikakis was at a low, because the return trip to Mikonos was much rougher than the outward journey. Shit, Angelos muttered.

Again, there was this question mark. Is my love for Khaled strong enough? I almost do not know him.

Then Angelos had to laugh.

I did not know Alex either. On the evening when they met for the first time, they had sex just four hours later. And married within a week.

Good. It's on trial and I do not want to separate from Alex. Not yet. But Alex had changed. The prickling, the cynicism on the one hand. On the other hand, Alex' love had something idolizing from the beginning. That's great at first, but it becomes a burden.

The carousel in Angelos´ head started spinning again.

7

Only twenty flying minutes away, Nikos Kyriakos was sitting at the kitchen table. His inconspicuous wife and his two overweight children pounced over the stuffed grape leaves that Nikos' mother regularly brought along. She knew that Nikos' wife was a lousy cook. One point on the negative list which his mother repeatedly presented. Nikos could not hear it anymore. Eleni is mediocre, just like me.
On the way up on the ladder of success, following the shriek of a vagina and immediately devoured: pregnant, marry and two children - that was the result of three years that had thrown Nikos off the track.
He had to bury his plans to become an archaeologist. The only thing which had ever really interested him was stolen from him. Studying was out of the question with a pregnant woman. He secretly resented Eleni. If I only would not have dropped down the pants, then today, I would...

The curse of the famous three minutes that only heterosexual men know - and pay for. The curse that gay men can not succumb by birth - for which they should be very grateful. But Nikos had no luck in this regard.
He envied his brother, because he was single and therefore could continue studying. The

little brother who had overtaken the big one. I will sit on my chair in the Ministry of Culture forever. If the post will not be rationalized. When Antonis told him that he was going to Delos, Nikos could not sleep at night.

I should have been happy about his luck, after all, he's my brother, Nikos thought, but I cannot.

And so, he broke off contact with Antonis. Nikos could not stand it. The constant stories of a place where he would have liked to be. And then came the day when a hitherto unknown man entered his office to inform himself about export certificates. The conversation lasted a good two hours and even at the end, Nikos was not clear which nationality his visitor was. He suspected Polish or Romanian.

But the visit changed his prospects. Not only that he would be able to leave this dreadful office, but at least he would get rid of the gnawing financial worries - and the constant trepidation of his wife, which blamed him for her modest lifestyle.

But for this quantum leap Nikos needed the help of his brother. Antonis, on the other hand, was horrified when Nikos carefully explained what it was all about. The conversation went into roar. Words such as traitor and criminal felt and Antonis stormed out of the café in Athens where they had met.

But two days later, Antonis was back. He had realized that his life was also at a dead end and agreed to the deal. But as it is. Once you have tasted blood, you cannot stop the greed. Of course, it wasn't only one deal, there were several and even if Antonis expressed his concerns again and again: they were not meant seriously but served only the own salvation.

If it will go wrong, Antonis would succeed in dumping all the blame on Nikos and presenting himself as a victim.

"Where is this idiot?", Nikos asked, after trying - in vain - to reach Antonis on his cell phone.

He did not know that the cell phone and its owner had already been pulverized.

He did not notice that he asked that question aloud and that Eleni heard it.

"I do not understand why you have so much yearning for your brother. You could not stand him for years. You did not even want to invite him for Christmas. Probably because he made his way - unlike you", etched Nikos' wife.

I would have become successful if I would not have made that terrible mistake to marry you, Nikos thought.

"He is part of the family. End of the discussion", Nikos said in a fit of courage.

It was already the second day without a sign of life, which was very unusual. In addition, Nikos had something urgent to discuss with Antonis.

Maybe a pillar felt on his head, Nikos thought for fun.
Well, that was close to reality.

8

A dam Resniak could hardly wait any longer. Six months had passed since he had left Salonika head over heels. In order not to leave unnecessary traces, he had initially bought no property, which would have resulted in an appointment with a notary and various bank transfers. All under a false name, but you should not take unnecessary risks in this business segment. And so, he rented a small apartment for three months and paid cash in advance. In many other countries this would cause an astonished look on - but not in Greece. The landlord was happy and promised Resniak not to disturb him if possible. The legend of the writer who seeks peace for writing his new book was usable again and again. It explains why the resident does not work at fixed times and some other behavior that deviates from the norm. And it should be considered that most authors write under a pseudonym, which makes research virtually impossible. Over the six months, Resniak had reconsidered his situation. For a final retirement, he was too young. He would have to *do* something and apart from his job he didn´t have any work experience. He struggled with himself whether he should contact his first agency again. He did not believe that they were responsible for his assassination – or better: the attempt. He smiled. Their orders were all small. But they were in the long term not lucrative enough and so he accepted orders from other suppliers. It was one of those, Adam believed. And so, he cautiously contacted his first "recruitment agency". They were more than pleased to hear from him. Obviously, his last failure had not spread. And so, he got a new job – or mission - immediately, with a little risk. He felt his spirits returning. Finally, he could do again what he was most satisfied with:

Killing people.

Shortly thereafter, Resniak made a second decision: he would settle down on Mikonos, whatever this means in case of a professional killer. He liked the island and above all: the possibility to flee in any direction at any time. For this purpose, he rented made a small, unobtrusive recreational boat.

Why didn´t I have the idea to live on Mikonos before?

9

When Angelos Nikakis arrived at home in Ornos, a van blocked his parking lot. For weeks craftsmen had worked in the neighboring house, which made the partly dilapidated house habitable again – in Greek speed. In other words, work was usually done from eight to twelve, in the afternoon at reduced speed. What Angelos understood: Working on a roof in the blazing heat - I'm not taking any!

Growling, he parked the SUV near the stadium around the corner and walked to the house.

"I think we see our new neighbor for the first time today", he told Alex, pointing to the window.

"Main thing: no kids", Alex answered succinctly. And in fact, a short while later, the new neighbor drove up in a nondescript Citroen.

"At least none of the VIP-scene, otherwise he would drive another car!"

Now Alex came to the window and looked at the new man next door.

"Gay?", he asked.

"Pooh. Alone, I guess in the late thirties.
If so, then one of the harder sorts", Angelos answered.

The man carried a box into the house, and you could see that he had strong muscles.

"No beauty. Look at the hair on his arms and back", Angelos said.

"Should I ever get hair on my back, shoot me, please", he added.

"I have a few, too", Alex said.

"Right. But when I saw it for the first time, it was already too late", Angelos grinned.

"That´s your own fault. Nobody forced you to sleep with me in the first night!"

"It was the first hour. You hardly allowed me to speak! "

"Do you regret it?", Alex asked and could have beaten his tongue.

Angelos couldn´t keep a straight face.

"In such moments: yes!"

Alex tried to change the subject quickly.

"What about the corpse?"

"What should be with it? At least half is missing. Look out. Wind Strength 7, you cannot do anything. You are from here!"

"Let us try again tomorrow", Alex suggested.

"Glad you still say 'us'!" Angelos countered.

"Do you already have a name?"

"Yes. Antonis Kyriakos. Archaeologist. Unfortunately, I still do not have the associated face", Angelos said.

'I do not have'. Aha, Alex thought.

The crack exists and is getting bigger.

10

I t was quiet in the car when Alex and Angelos drove to the harbor for taking the boat to Delos island.

The wind had dropped significantly. So, they and the director of the archaeological parc walked from the new pier to the antique theater.

"The.., uh, body parts must be taken away immediately. They start to stink.

Unacceptable to visitors and employees", growled Papadopoulos.

"I think Mr. Kyriakos also considers his state as critical". Who wants to be disassembled into forty pieces? You?", Angelos replied snappy.

"I cannot feel any compassion. He does not come back either. But I cannot accept another one-day visit ban. Otherwise, the community will go through the roof. Oh, that's YOU!", Papadopoulos answered.

Idiot, Angelos thought.

"You can reopen tomorrow. Can we turn to the scene right now?", Angelos asked.

Papadopoulos nodded and they reached the theater.

The ancient theater of Delos was one of the better-preserved buildings - or rather, ruins. Stage, parts of the columns and the first two rows of seats were still clearly identifiable.

"Why are there backrests in the front row?"
Alex asked.

"For the better people – or VIPs as we would
call them. The common people sat on
benches", Angelos replied, who of course
had to know Delos as mayor.

"To my shame, I must confess: I was only once
on Delos. And I was born here", Alex said a bit
meekly.

"Peasant", Angelos answered, but smiled
broadly.

"So, Mr. Papadopoulos, we need your help.
How looked the ruin before and what was
destroyed by the explosion?", Alex asked.

"The starting point of the explosion was
probably here, in the area of the rearmost
rows. It seems so", Angelos interrupted. The
day before, you really could not see anything
through wind and dust.

"In some parts of the corpse there are
splinters. But wood can hardly be 3,000 years
old.

Especially not with varnish", Angelos said with
a grin.

"Most colleagues have wooden boxes in their
areas. Their devices are in it. Brushes and so
on,", Papadopoulos replied.

"So, the bomb was probably in that toolbox",
Alex stated. "Who has keys for the boxes?"

"Only the person concerned. But these are
just normal padlocks. They should only
prevent tourists from taking souvenirs. Normal

brushes, as you can buy in any hardware store. Incomprehensible."

"Oh, you know, there are people who pay for worn underpants, even though new one´s are cheaper", Angelos replied.

"Your prince, perhaps?", Papadopoulos asked with a grin.

With some difficulty Alex could prevent Angelos from beating Papadopoulos.

Angry, Angelos went two rows forward, bent down and held something indefinable in his hand.

"Look, Alex. A testicle of Mr. Kyriakos!" Papadopoulos had to vomit. And not just once.

"That was not nice", Alex whispered into Angelos´ ear. "What is it really?"

"I think, tissue parts of a thigh!"

"I better go now", said a deranged Papadopoulos.

"I will pay him back in kind", Angelos scolded.

"And? Is it true? Does Khaled have worn panties from you?", Alex asked.

"It's none of your business", Angelos growled.

"You are so right. I'm only your husband!"

"Marital conflict or crime scene inspection?", Angelos asked.

Alex preferred the crime scene inspection.

11

The return trip was mostly quiet.
"Family?", Alex asked shortly.
"Giorgios says Kyriakos has a brother in Athens", Angelos replied.
"Call or drive?"
"Would you like to get a call that your brother was dissected into forty pieces?"
"Shall I come with you?", Alex asked.
"No. Think better about whether you want to reproach me something for all eternity, to which you have given your consent!"
"I agreed to one night. Not that you fall in love", Alex retorted.
"You think you can control love? Then think about our first day", Angelos growled.

When they got home, they saw the new neighbor closing their garden door and walking back to his house.
"Oh dear, welcome visit", Alex said.
At least the bottle of wine in the hand of the neighbor pointed it out. And in fact, he came to the two commissioners.
"Buon giorno. Or better: Jassas! I'm Marco Tardelli, your new neighbor. I thought I should introduce myself!"
Tardelli wore jeans and a T-shirt. Despite the shirt, the hair spilled out of the neck.
"Well then, welcome", Angelos said
and the three went inside.

"Espresso? An Italian does not need anything else, does he? ", Alex asked.

Tardelli laughed.

"Right. Stylishly decorated", he said and entered the kitchen.

He looked shocked when he saw the eight monitors on the wall.

"So, either you're a stalker couple or you work for the secret service", he said.

Angelos laughed.

"Nearly. Somehow commissioners are stalkers. And by the way, I am the mayor of this crazy island. But do not think you could ring us when the power goes off.

I'm not on duty before twelve o'clock", Angelos replied.

"The Italian way. I like that", the neighbor said.

"Two men in a house. Gay?"

Angelos took Alex in his arms and kissed him on the cheek.

"Further questions?"

Tardelli laughed again.

"Like-minded people. The difference is that I am alone. But I would like to change that!"

"Then there is no better place than Mikonos", Angelos said.

"Any tips?"

"Oh dear. We are, 'withdrawn from the market'. The beach for older people is 'Elia'. And in the beach clubs you will only find young boys. The classic bars are in the Chora", Alex replied.

"Well then, good neighborhood. I have to prepare for the first night tour!"
Then he disappeared.
"Nice", Angelos said.
"Hairy", Alex replied.

12

A few days later, Angelos flew alone to Athens to visit Antonis Kyriakos' brother, deliver the bad news and learn more about the tattered victim.
The questioning of the colleagues did not produce anything useful and took hours.
Angelos Nikakis hated Athens. For him it was a crime scene, the place where he had been raped. Trips to Athens, cannot be completely avoided both as a commissioner and as a mayor, he reduces it to the minimum. He detoured the quarter where it all happened.
Thankfully, Nikos Kyriakos's apartment in Rafina, east of the city, was far enough away from ... Angelos got goose bumps and the images of that day reappeared in his mind. The taxi with the inevitable African driver stopped in front of a shabby skyscraper, a bunker from the sixties.
Whatever Nikos did professionally, his salary cannot be high.

The apartment door opened, and he saw a face in the forties with narrow lips, alarm signal number 1 for every man. As if she had already guessed, she said:

"You look like police. Just walk in. Take him with you. No matter for what!"

She steered Angelos into the kitchen and shouted across the flat:

"Nikos! Kitchen! Police!"

Angelos already felt sorry for him and it did not get better when Nikos entered the kitchen.

He was the walking misery.

"Angelos Nikakis, CID Mikonos!"

Kyriakos was not surprised.

"CID Mikonos? Then you are the commissar with the prince? My brother told me.

God - I envy you ... ", he said surprisingly.

Angelos was perplexed.

"Why?"

"Did not you see and hear my wife? You can only become gay when you have such a ...! "

As if he would have known it, the door opened and the angry face of his wife appeared:

"Oh, Commissioner, one more thing: Use only simple sentences. He does not understand anything else!"

She slammed the door.

"My condolences", Angelos said. "No escape possible?"

"Children," Nikos answered with resignation.

"Well, at least I was spared from this", Angelos said. "But I'm not here because of your marital problems, but because of your brother!
I'm sorry to tell you he's dead! "
Nikos Kyriakos looked a little astonished but said nothing at first.
But his wife looked back into the kitchen. Of course, she had listened.
"I knew it. Your great and so successful brother. He had a skeleton on his closet", she snapped.
"Get out of here," roared Angelos, and surprisingly, the woman let herself be thrown out of her own kitchen.
"Can you not stay for a while?", Nikos asked. There was silence.
"Antonis. He has a better life. Or had. Solo. Could do what he wanted. And could choose his dream job. Archaeologist. And this on Delos. That was originally my dream. But instead of Xanthippe as a statue I got her alive. Poor Antonis. I suppose it was an accident?"
Death on Mikonos normally means traffic accident.
Angelos shook his head.
"He was killed by an explosion", Angelos said.
"In the house?", was the legitimate question.
"No. On Delos", Angelos answered.
Nikos became a living question mark.
"What is going to explode there? A gas bottle?"

Angelos shook his head again.

"It was a bomb in your brother's toolbox. He should be killed purposefully!"

"A murder? You make jokes. He was an archaeologist!", Nikos said.

"Precisely. He had no enemies on the island. He was also popular among colleagues. The next to ask is the family. How was your relationship to your brother? "

"After the wedding we only saw each other sporadically. I'm honest: I was jealous of him and could not bear to see how he could do what I was denied. But I told myself: he is not responsible and he's my brother. Or was. Anyway, I contacted him again and then he visited me every two months. When he talked about Delos, I was stung, but I was in control. So, I had no quarrel with him. Others? I do not think so. He was a jovial guy. Just like me, before I ... well ... you know! Who is responsible for the funeral? "

"You're the next relative", Angelos said, noticing that Nikos looked dizzy.

"Oh God, how should I pay for that?"

"I think a normal funeral is canceled. He does not look too good", Angelos said carefully.

"What does that mean?"

"He consists of 45 parts, but we have not yet found all. The head is still missing!"

At that moment, Nikos slipped off the chair. Angelos called to Nikos's wife, who remained completely unaffected by her unconscious husband. She poured a cup of water into his face.

"How affectionate", Angelos growled.

"I knew that this would happen. Something is rotten here. From one moment to the other the two loved each other again and met very often.

"Shut up," smirked Nikos, who gained back consciousness.

"Can you perhaps explain to me what your wife meant?"

"I have not the slightest idea. She does not like it when I talk to others at all. "

"You make your living from …?", Angelos asked, realizing that Nikos had a hard time answering.

"I work in the Ministry of Culture!"

"A little bit more accurate?", Angelos asked.

"I am responsible for export certificates for antique objects. But not alone. I'm just putting the stamp on it!"

"Antique objects? Exported?", Angelos asked in surprise. "They belong to Greek museums!"

Nikos smiled.

"Oh, Commissioner. You are not a specialist, for which I do not blame you. It happens that foreign museums buy artifacts. Some can only be restored abroad. There are also exhibitions all over the world. And then there are items that are sold on the open market just because there are thousands of them. They have no value. What do you think, how many amphorae are found in Greece daily?

They are worthless, archaeologically, and still bring money into the country!"

At bottom logical explanations, but Commissioner Nikakis still had that intuitively feeling which is typical for policemen.

The victim: archaeologist.

The brother: In the Ministry responsible for export licenses. Funny coincidence.

"All right. That's it for now. An identification of the body is not necessary because Antonis' DNA was already matched. The casket will be delivered to you in the next days!"

By UPS. Open carefully, otherwise Antonis will be spread all over the kitchen, Angelos would have liked to add, but he stopped timely.

When Angelos wanted to leave the apartment, the other door opened again. Nikos' wife.

"Do not believe a word. There was something between the two!"

Angelos left.

Thank god I'm gay. I would have killed her already and the sentence would not be more than a speeding ticket.

13

The interview did not take as long as expected, because at first Angelos needed more information about the work of Nikos Kyriakos and he would not get it from himself. At least not the decisive details.

If the taxi driver hurries, I'll even catch the 1.00- pm-flight, Angelos thought.

To Angelos' surprise, Volotea sent him directly to the gate and he did not have to pay.

"Since when Volotea is so generous?"

"Because we hope you and your prince will fly with us in the future. It makes no sense to use a Learjet from Mikonos to Athens!"

The lady at the check-in was also in the Tower on the evening, when Khaled landed on Mikonos. Among fifty others.

"Would Volotea like to take a picture of us?" Angelos asked irritably.

"Volotea maybe not. But I would like to have one! Have a good flight!"

Angelos landed at 1:35 pm and thought for a moment whether he should go to the town hall, but since he had no appointments, he decided to go home.

Hc parkcd a little further away from the house. At this time all citizens of Ornos seemed to go shopping - the biggest supermarket was just a few blocks away. On his short walk he saw the neighbor's car. I

hope he does not see me, Angelos thought.
He did not feel like small talk.

He entered the house and was astonished:
Alex was not there. He usually does the
paperwork from noon on, checks the
cameras - and watches the fuss in the old
town on the monitors. Much more effective
than patrols. And more comfortable.

Espresso, Angelos thought, but the water tank
was empty. When he wanted to fill it, only
drops came out of the tap.

Wonderful.

Once again, the hose of the tank had
loosened because the clamp was not the
newest one. The problem: the tank was on
the roof and the only way up was with a
ladder.

Angelos cursed. He went outside, picked up
the ladder and leaned it against the wall.
When he reached the top, he saw the mess.
The clamp broke off completely and Angelos
was standing in a pool of water. He decided
to take two minutes to breathe and leaned
against the tank. A nice view, he thought.
And then he had a kind of "apparition".

He saw Alex, wearing only a towel, emerging
from the neighbor's garden shed and running
behind the house.

The process took less than two minutes. At
first, Angelos thought his brain was playing a
dirty trick on him. A Fata Morgana Greco, so
to speak. But shortly thereafter the neighbor
left the garden shed. Unlike Alex, he was in

no hurry. He didn´t wear clothes too, not even a towel. You could admire him in "full hair". Ok - he could not guess that Angelos was standing on the roof.

For whatever reason, Angelos pulled out his phone and took some pictures.

Tardelli stretched and smiled.

It was clear what had happened in the shed. Angelos was paralyzed.

Alex and this primate?

Carefully he climbed down the stairs. The water tank had become unimportant.

Angelos went to the kitchen. Next espresso. Triple.

He cheated on me. Let's see if he lies to me too. I never did either, Angelos thought. He should have been desperate, but he was not. And yet there was no anger. There was only emptiness.

Ten minutes later Alex came through the door.

"Agapi-mou, what are you doing here?"

He kissed Angelos on the head.

Angelos shook it.

"How was your day?", Alex asked.

"Good. I've been to Kyriakos in Athens and I have a clue what it's all about. Well and then I fixed the water tank on the roof!"

Alex´ espresso cup dropped down.

"You know, from up there you have a nice view!"

"On what?", Alex pressed out.

"For example, the beach and the neighboring house!"

"Yeah, uh, Tardelli invited me for a coffee", Alex said, but without looking at Angelos.

Aha. I did not know you have to put your trunk in the cup to drink", Angelos said quietly. He cheated on me. And lied.

"And then with this gorilla, whose hair grows out of his nose and ears!"

"Not everyone can be as beautiful as you", Alex growled.

"Is that your justification?"

"You first slept with someone else", Alex switched to attack.

'That was different. Khaled saved our lives. Plural. Including yours! Already forgotten? Ten seconds later we would have got a head shot. And he just wished for a night with me, he did not demand it. And I told you. I did not just do it. I ASKED you and you said yes. With a 'no' I would not have done it. So, I did not cheat or lie to you! "

Alex sat down at the table and buried his face in his hands.

"Again: no further explications?", Angelos asked.

"What can I say? I only consented to the sex. But not that you fall in love with him. You're my man! Do you know how much I suffered? Expecting daily that you run to your sheikh!", Alex spoke loudly.

"How many times have I told you that I'm staying with you, Khaled, Khaled? Where have I been the whole time? HERE! With my husband!"

"But how long? Something is different than before!"

Angelos laughed sardonically.

"You are right. My husband lied to me and went to bed with a monkey from the neighborhood. Stop! No, it was the garden shed. You should take a quick shower, not that all his hair is sticking", roared Angelos.

"I never cheated on you. Not once. Although you've alleged me several times. There was never anything", Angelos said, now a little quieter.

"Do you think I did?", Alex objected.

Angelos laughed.

"And what was that today? If only it had been with André!"

André was the chief director of the clinic, who was clearly in love with Alex and therefore could not stand Angelos.

"I do not know either. Tardelli is not good-looking. It was probably the frustration. I'm sorry", Alex said softly.

"I can't hear it anymore, this 'I'm sorry'". You must think before you do something. Nothing but bad excuses!"

After that there was silence in the Nikakis house.

"Now, I'll go upstairs and pack a few things. Everything else will be settled in the next few days,", Angelos said.

At first Alex did not understand the significance and the consequences of the incident.

"Angelos, please. I beg you ...!"

But Angelos did not say anything.

"So, you'll run back to your sheikh", Alex roared upstairs.

Angelos was running out of the bedroom.

"His name is KHALED. And he loves me. He does not betray me. Especially not with an ugly brush!"

Angelos stormed down the stairs and left the house.

Slowly the incident reached Alex' brain and it decided to switch off.

Alex fainted.

14

Angelos did not remain untouched by the struggle. On the roof he felt: nothing. Was it just the shock? And now the world collapsed on him:

Would I misuse Khaled if I call him now?

Are my feelings for Khaled enough for a happy relationship?

Do I have to resign as mayor?

How should the investigation work be done in the future? By whom?

Does that work with two divorced commissioners at all?

Do I want a divorce?

Again, it shook him at the thought of Alex and the hairy neighbor.

The happy days seemed distant. Far away the Alex, who did everything for him. Maybe that was the reason for the end. The way Alex adored Angelos had to turn one day into the opposite.

And then, a third man appeared.

Khaled.

Angelos did not know if he should curse this day. Or should I be grateful, Angelos wondered.

He took a deep breath, started the engine, but whereto?

No matter. Away from here. I do not want to see Alex running to the gorilla.

Angelos drove to Kalafati and parked the car above the bay. It was his favorite place on Mikonos.

He had to decide. Call Khaled or live alone for a while?

It did not take him three seconds to admit he could not be alone.

Maybe a consequence of his rape.

He reached for his cell phone:

MY SHEIK. IT HAPPENED. WE HAVE SEPARATED. WOULD LOVE TO SEE YOU. I AM COMPLETELY CONFUSED. NATURALLY ONLY, IF YOU STILL WANT TO. ANGELOS.

Maybe he met a new guy.

At Khaled's age, 25, that happens fast. Angelos grinned, thinking that now HE would be the elder in the relationship. Nearly five years difference, as with him and Alex, only that Alex was the elder in their marriage. Desperate he looked at the sea.

15

K haled was thunderstruck. THIS was the decisive moment of his life; he was absolutely sure.

Then the SMS penetrated to the last corner of his brain. And Khaled screamed out his joy! There is no way back. I will do everything exactly as I have imagined since I met Angelos Nikakis.

The resignation. The break-up with the family. The waiver of luxury.

ONLY IF YOU WANT TO, Angelos had written. Khaled thought something fishy is going on. I have to be careful, so nothing goes wrong. Now that a dream has come true, A dream, I did not believe that it will become reality. The bond between Alex and Angelos seemed too strong.

But it was a warning: Khaled, you must always be vigilant and not idolize Angelos. That was probably Alex' mistake. And had to lead to ruin.

Khaled got goose bumps at the thought of sleeping with Angelos every night from now on. A wave of energy spilled through his body.

Now, I must find the right words.

MY PRINCE CHARMING. FINALLY. I AM THE HAPPIEST MAN IN THE WORLD. I AM ON THE WAY. HANG IN THERE. I LOVE YOU. KHALED.

And now I must leave right away. But I am in the middle of the Negev desert. In a country where I should not be.

He went to the room of the agents of the Israeli intelligence service.

"Gentlemen, I have to interrupt the talks. There are only private reasons, there is no political background. But ..."

One of the men smiled.

"You must fly to Mikonos urgently. Am I right?"

Khaled derailed the face.

"Who ..."

"Oh, come on. We are a secret service; we MUST know something like that!"

The man opened a dossier and took out a photo.

"Angelos Nikakis. A beauty. And clever. At least our friends from the Greek secret service say so. Has he finally said yes?"

Khaled nodded.

'Then we'll bring you to Amman right away. From there you can fly with your jet to Mikonos. You want to leave immediately?"

Khaled nodded vigorously.

God, he is nuts about Nikakis, thought the man of the SERVICE, as the Israeli secret service is usually called.

He felt sorry for Khaled. His family would break with him. A wave of hate will hit him and not just an ordinary shitstorm.

But we still need this man. Maybe we should accompany him, at least discreetly.

'Then, Royal Highness: good luck!"

16

Angelos was happy too and he finally admitted it. No consideration anymore. Set your feelings free.

And yes. I love Khaled. But it will not be easy. Khaled is - still – a person of public interest. I'm less important, but ... I hope we can handle it.

I WILL BE THERE IN THREE HOURS. JOY ABOUT OUR FIRST NIGHT AS A REAL COUPLE.

Angelos smiled. Are we really a real couple? Yes, we will be. I am sure.

At the airport: same sort as usual, when the news arrives that an aircraft under diplomatic immunity would land out of schedule on JMK.

Although there were enough politicians and celebrities to land on Mikonos, *their* jets usually do not have an Emirati identifier. And besides, it was the same label as last time when the Crown Prince arrived at the airport. Still, not all islanders had seen the Crown Prince and the Mayor live and so the tower was filling up in no time.

A few hours later the time has come. You could hear the roar of engines, a very different sound than from conventional passenger aircrafts.

Shortly thereafter, the jet stopped and took his parking position: right in front of the tower. Curious pack, Angelos thought, they lead the jet directly under the tower, so that they can see everything.

The engines stopped. And then he came out. From the off you could hear a female voice. "Welcome to Mikonos, Royal Highness. Please do not take our mayor with you, we still need him!"

Angelos stretched his middle finger towards the Tower and then kissed Khaled. No welcome kiss like the last few times, but a violent kiss, in which all the pent-up feelings of the past months unloaded. Then something strange happened. Khaled and Angelos went onboard of the plane and shortly thereafter the crew came out: two pilots, the flight attendant and two security men.

Then the door closed again.

A minute later, Angelos´ voice was heard in the Tower:

"You will not do the following things: to spray the plane with extinguishing foam or to move it with the pusher, otherwise you will be sweeping the beach tomorrow!"

You could hear loud laughter in the tower.

"We would never do that", said the air traffic controller.

"You would!"

Angelos left the cockpit and went into the cabin, where Khaled was already getting rid of his jeans.

"Your Royal Highness is in a hurry", Angelos said.

"The Royal Highness has been waiting for six weeks", Khaled replied.

"No one else?"

Khaled looked at Angelos dumbfounded.

"Did you?"

"No. Not even with Alex", Angelos said.

"May I ask the mayor to follow me to the shower!"

Hopefully the plane will not wobble, or we'll find ourselves on "You Tube" tomorrow, Angelos thought.

Obviously, the jet moved, because from the outside you could hear powerful basses:

"Push it!"

"Well, these idiots at least have humor", Angelos said.

Twenty Minutes (and 6 Times "Push it") later:

With smiling faces, Khaled and Angelos sat in the leather seats.

"Now please tell me what happened", Khaled said.

Angelos described this memorable day, which - unexpectedly - ended in the Crown Prince's jet.

Although Royal Highness would soon be nor 'royal' neither 'highness' anymore.

"HE DID WHAT? Cheated you with the neighbor? That's like in q bad movie", Khaled replied.

"By the way, the neighbor is no beauty. He is ..uh, well, very hairy", Angelos growled.

"Well, I'm lucky", Khaled said, grinning. He had only little hair on his legs.

"I know, it looks like I'm going to use you as a fill-in because I cannot be alone, but ..." Angelos began.

"A fill-in? The 'fill-in' has hoped for months that this happens. I waited for this day, I lived for it. Now this day has come. At least I hope so. I do not know yet what your plans are!"

"What am I planning to do? Does the welcome ceremony leave any questions unanswered? Alex and the neighbor just accelerated it a bit, which would have happened anyway. The last weeks were only the swan song. I love you. And I want to be with you", Angelos said.

Khaled got up, went into the cockpit and cried into the microphone: "Hooray!"

Angelos laughed.

"Hopefully they will not play the wedding march now!"

And after a short break, he added:

"Are you sure? That you can live with a normal man? Without all the luxury and crown prince stuff?"

Khaled laughed.

"If I am sure? Hi? I flew to Mikonos the second time after a cry for help from you. And does not my face say everything?"

And indeed: Khaled's eyes were shining.

"But we will live a normal life. I'm a small mayor and we need to find employment for you, otherwise you would stalk young men all day!"

"My name is not Alex. He will also have promised you to be faithful, but I will always be. Trust me and just look into my eyes!"

"Does that mean we try it together?", Angelos asked.

"No. Trying is too little. I will do more. And you too", Khaled replied.

"Then all I hope is that I will never get a hairy neighbor again" flattest Angelos.

"But fierce days will come. You have to tell your dad, it will go through the media, they will scold you. Is it worth it? Am I worth it?"

"A thousand times, yes!", said a smiling Khaled.

"Practical question: we need ..."

"Everything is already done. You mean a hotel?"

Khaled wiped his cell phone.

"Villas del Mar in Agios whatsoever!"
Angelos rolled his eyes.
"Agios Ioannis. The most expensive villas of
the island. I think 9,000 euros per night. Did
not we want to live a normal life? "
Khaled smiled.
"May I please enjoy my luck for a few days?
In addition, I have been assured that the
villas are hermetically shielded by a security
service!"
"You won the set. Do we agree on a
maximum of two weeks in which we look for
something normal?"
"You mean without own concierge and
without own chef de cuisine? Phew. It's going
to be hard", Khaled said and laughed.
"My cooking skills are limited".
"You can learn that, Royal Highness", Angelos
answered.

17

Angelos lolled in bed.
Khaled came out of the shower, where a heater fan made bath towels superfluous.

What a beautiful man, Angelos thought.

The full lips, the wide but not bushy eyebrows, those bright green eyes. Not to mention the body.

Angelos pulled a pout.

"I never thought I would ever say that. But you are actually more beautiful than me. Blow! "

Khaled bent with laughter.

"My humbled mayor. But I can assure you: I am not a competition for you. I know that everyone is watching you. Women AND men. And you know that!"

Khaled lay down next to Angelos.

"I cannot get enough of you!"

Angelos smiled.

"I hope that will be the same in a year's time!"

"I'm not Alex. I will look next to me every day after waking up and thank for my happiness", Khaled said.

"Heavens, you are a word artist!", Angelos answered with a laugh.

A shadow flew over Angelos' face.

"You're thinking of Alex, aren´t you?", Khaled asked.

"Are you a clairvoyant too? Sorry, I'm a bit worried. He has said so many times that he cannot live without me ... "

"... and put you under pressure", Khaled added.

"Well, I think it is true!"

"Aha. Then why is he sleeping with the neighbor?", Khaled asked.

"I think it was a kind of revenge for falling in love with you", Angelos said.

"What you could not control. You thought with your heart, but Alex thought with his ... And I did not do anything to disperse you", Khaled replied.

"Except that you showered me with so much flattery that I had to fall into the honey pot like a bee. In an exceptionally beautiful pot, I should probably add, and even in a royal!"

Angelos grinned and kissed Khaled.

"Well, that 'royal' will disappear soon. When are you going to get your things from Alex?"

Angelos put the pillow over his face.

"Do not say you're not sure anymore", Khaled said, startled.

Angelos threw the pillow on the floor and stroked Khaled over the head.

"My royal idiot. I do not change my mind every week. Remember that.

But it will hurt when I see Alex. Everything else would be abnormal. Although there is not much to fix. He gets my half of the house and I do not want anything else either", Angelos said.

"That's very generous of you", Khaled replied. "But the job becomes a problem. So far, we have determined together because we are both Commissioners. Whether that still works, I do not know. But what else should Alex do? Leaving Mikonos where he was born? Because of me? No way!"

"Maybe he'll move to the hairy neighbor. Should he take care of Alex! "

After a short pause, Khaled added:

"No. That was unfair. Excuse me. Everything can stay as it is for me. Even if I have the worry that ... "

"... that I end up in bed with him? You mean that?"

"I'm honest: yes", Khaled said meekly.

"I have NEVER ever betrayed him. And I will not do it with you either. Enough. That´s it!"

"Forgive me, my sweetheart. I trust you fully and you can trust me. I have not even looked at another man since I met you", Khaled said, and his eyes shone again.

"Which explains why you cannot get enough. If you just touch my best pieces today, they will fall off", Angelos replied.

"No sex today? I cannot stand that", protested Khaled.

"Well, a little round maybe ...", Angelos said. "When will you tell your father?"

"I'm even more afraid of that than you are before meeting Alex. I will be in the middle of a shitstorm. Not just on the net, but especially on TV!"

Once again, Angelos realized what Khaled was giving up and risking.

An Arab prince who is gay. And, moreover, having a relationship with a Greek. He will not miss the luxury, because I'm enough for him, Angelos thought.

"We gonna make it. Everyone out there can kiss our ass, or asses", he said. "In addition, we determine the time of publication!"

Angelos should be wrong.

Because only an hour later it started.

18

T he breakfast was served. By the butler. Prepared by their own cook.

"This must stop. One week! ", protested Angelos.

"I promised. We're looking for something small and cute this week", Khaled replied.

"I can imagine what you mean by 'cute'", Angelos said with a laugh.

"But you're not my sugar daddy, especially since you're younger than me", Angelos added with a grin.

"It will be a completely new life for you. I hope you understand that. You can still ... "

"Can I do what? To pull back? Are you crazy? I could also move to a lonely island without any comfort, just with you!"

Khaled was taken aback.

"A lonely island? What would we do there all day? Sex? Then I would be dead after a month because you are a greedy monster, That is what you are!", Angelos taunted.

"Sorry, I have a lot to catch up with. If it gets too much for you, then ... "

Angelos shook his head.

"It was a joke. I'm 30 and not 50!", he said.

That he was now the older in the relationship, was strange for Angelos.

"Does a normal house have a butler and a pool?", Khaled asked with a grin.

"NO", Angelos said. "Although: a small pool would be nice. But only a small one. No lake landscape like here!"

"You decide. Basta. I would never have dreamed that I ever say something like that. Nobody decides something for a Crown Prince. Ok, except my dad", Khaled replied.

"Seriously. We buy the house that you like. It's enough for me to be with you!"

Angelos smiled.

Hopefully it will work. It's a dream so far, but what about in a year? Will he be bored with me?

"And that will never change", Khaled said just then.

"Tell me, Prince of 1001 Nights, can you read minds?" Angelos asked.

"Just call me Aladdin. But I have no magic lamp, but a miraculous ...! "

Angelos snorted.

"The miraculous thing is more of a torture device, but a beautiful one, my Aladdin!"

After breakfast Angelos took his notebook.
"OH HOLY SHIT!", he shouted.
"What is?"
"Read that!"
Angelos handed Khaled the notebook.
On the side of Al-Jazeera stood as Headline:
CROWN PRINCE OF FUDCHEIRAH GAY.
SECRET RELATIONSHIP WITH GREEK MAYOR.
NO REACTION FROM PALACE. EXPERTS
EXPECT WITHDRAWAL AS CROWN PRINCE
KHALED.
Khaled was pale and unable to speak.
Angelos put his arm around him and said softly:
"You will stay my prince. And we gonna make it together. They will not succeed in destroying us! No way!"
Khaled smiled weakly.
"Basically, I should be happy.
I have wished all that for such a long time. Especially the sentence with the Greek mayor. But I'm still afraid of my dad. He is callous and cruel. Hopefully they will not involve you!"
"You do not believe that yourself. We both stand there with our trousers down", Angelos said.
Khaled laughed.
"A nice idea!"

But to keep Angelos out of the trouble will be an illusion.

"Oh shit", Khaled said, reading.

CROWNPRINCE WANTS TO MARRY HIS LOVER, MAYOR ANGELOS NIKAKIS OF MIKONOS. SECRET MEETING FOR MONTHS. NIKAKIS IS MARRIED, BUT SOON DIVORCED.

Angelos looked annoyed.

"So? We want to marry? Like always they know more than those affected. And Alex will collapse! Fuck!"

"Did not you want to be divorced?", Khaled asked.

"Khaled, honestly, I have not had time to think about it yet. My brain is already getting hot!"

Khaled struggled with himself.

"Angelos. Could you at least imagine marrying me? "

Angelos hesitated.

"My first attempt was not very successful", Angelos replied, "but before you get depressed unnecessarily: yes, theoretically. But now we have completely different sorrows!"

"No. My biggest concern is that you ...!"

"Stop it! Do not start like Alex. I love you and hope it remains that way for a long time. From my sake until the end. Satisfied?"

Khaled smiled gratefully - and relieved.

"Definitely!"

There was not much time for them to catch their breath.

19

One of the security men of the villa complex appeared.

"There is a man outside. He says he works at the airport and urgently needs to talk to you, mayor. I tried to get rid of him, but ..."

"Alright", Angelos said. "He should come here!"

A visibly depressed man entered the lawn. He had no view for the luxury. Angelos knew him. It was Vassilis from the tower crew.

"Oh, I did not know ... Good morning, Royal Highness", Vassilis said.

"Whom do you mean? Him or me?", Angelos said and laughed.

Khaled grinned.

"Let's forget the 'Royal Highness'. You can tell the others same. I am just Khaled - hopefully Khaled Nikakis soon!"

He's serious, Angelos thought.

"Too friendly, Ro .., uh, Khaled. But you will not be so kind to me anymore", Vassilis replied, still looking at the floor.

"Just spit it out. The Emir has his gracious day today", Angelos said, using his nickname the whole island now used.

"Emir, I did something stupid. When you arrived at the airport yesterday and greeted Khaled, uh, I took some pictures!"

"And? There were certainly twenty men in the tower", Angelos said.

"There were even more. Well. I told my sister-in-law in Athens that, um, I do not want to offend you, you have a relationship with a real prince. The Emir and the prince. As from 1001 night. My sister-in-law did not believe me. So, I sent her one of the photos to prove it. One where you kiss each other. And this stupid cow sent this private photo to her friend who works for the television. I did not know that someone else sees the photo. I could kick myself. I am sorry!"

"Well, then we know at least the source Do not worry. If you had not done it, someone else would have sent the photos. This happened just a little bit faster than planned. But it honors you to come here to confess, Vassilis! Let's just forget it", Angelos said.

Vassilis beamed with relief.

"God, I'm relieved now. You should not be fooled with the Emir", he said with a smile. "But maybe I can wish you good luck. And again sorry, also to you, King .., er, Khaled "!

"It's okay", Angelos said, "and back to work now. And, Vassilis?"

"What, Emir?"

"I would like to see the pictures, please send them to my mobile phone", Angelos said.

Vassilis nodded.

"People like and respect you. The name is not so wrong. An Emir should be strict, but also kind", Khaled said.

Angelos laughed.

"Yeah, but the post of the Emir of Mikonos is badly paid!"

"Believe me, respect and affection are priceless", Khaled said.

"You're 25 years old and feed me one philosophical sentence after the other. But I'm just ... "

"... a small mayor and commissioner. You can leave that in the future. You are much more. You just do not believe it sometimes. You are not as self-confident as others think. I suppose it comes from the rape. I'm grateful to Alex for shooting one of those bastards. And to philosophy: I must have learned something in Harvard", Khaled said, smiling. "However, nobody has prepared me for this here. The perfect luck!"

I love him more every day, Angelos thought. I hope he has the strength to endure the storm that is coming.

Angelos kissed Khaled passionately.

"You smell like ..."

Khaled thought as Angelos rolled his eyes.

"Peach, right? Anyway, Alex always said that. And sometimes called me, my lillle peach'!"

Khaled laughed.

'That sounds a bit too gay. I stick to 'sweetheart' and 'beauty' if that suits you?"

'That fits perfectly", Angelos replied. "And by the way: it´s the truth!"
Both laughed.

Three miles away, a man was standing by the window and was not so relaxed.

20

The Emir of Fudscheirah stood at the large panorama window and stared on the hills. He had no view for the beauty of the mountains. Otherwise the view inspired him and gave him strength. But today?
It was a thing like that with the strength anyway. He had been told in the clinic in Dubai that he was suffering from pancreatic cancer. And the whole thing was already in an advanced stage. Inoperable.
All my money will not save me, the Emir thought. I am only 63 years old. No age to die. Nobody knew about, not even the other ruling families of the Emirates. Not to mention the population.
After a few days of shock, he understood that he now had to take more care of the question of his succession. He sat at his big desk and looked at the photos of his five children. He had three sons and two

daughters. The latter, of course, ruled out. A woman as Emir? He laughed loud.

He took the photos of his three sons and put them on his notebook.

Rashid, the oldest. A good-for-nothing. Big cars, drugs, women. Every night at a different party and what bothered the Emir the most: he was more in Dubai than here in his own Emirate. Not the best condition for rule over Fudscheirah. Had he ever been in the local mountains? Certainly not. There was no alcohol and no half-naked women. Painted.

Ahmed, the second born. A conceited idiot. Clearly, he is similar to his mother.

My own mother had warned me, the Emir thought. Do not be blinded by the beauty. Aicha was not even twenty and more than attractive. He was already 36 and his father had made it clear to him that he could forget the succession to the throne if he was still unmarried at the age of forty.

And since Aicha was a sight for sore eyes, the decision was easy. Unfortunately, I was the only one who did not know that Aicha was dumb. Not in the sense that she was uneducated. That was part of the educational principle how to handle daughters. No, it was clearly a lack of intelligence and it had transferred to Ahmed. So, he would fail, the Emir thought.

And then his pride: Khaled. Eloquent, educated and handsome. Of no small importance; the people loved him and would be happy if he became the new Emir. Studied in Harvard and always interested in state affairs and foreign policy. Several tricky missions had been managed by Khaled. When I got the diagnosis, the only consolation was that I could hand over the business to my youngest son, without worrying about my legacy.

Everything was clear, the Emir thought. Until this morning.

Until the head of his secret service appeared here and was beating for ten minutes about the bush. The Emir's collar busted. Only then Mansoor came out with the truth:

"Your Highness, Crown Prince Khaled is obviously, uh, uh, gay. That's when ... "

"I am old, but not stupid. I'm warning you!", the Emir said loudly.

After a short break he asked, although he already knew the answer.

"Khaled loves men? How can that be?"

"They are born that way. It is God's will", Mansoor replied, amazed by his own courage.

"The Koran prohibits sodomy, so it cannot be that ...", the Emir began.

The usual scheme, Mansoor thought. We have 5G in the country, but views from the 18th century. At some point, the whole Emirate will blow up in our face. Facebook, Twitter and Koran schools preaching Wahhabism. It will tear us apart.

"How do you know it? Are you sure? ", the Emir asked.

"Absolutely. It is broadcasted everywhere and my sources in Greece confirm the story!"

"My son loves men", the Emir muttered, as if he still could not believe it.

"No, Highness. He loves one man", Mansoor said.

"And who is this subject?"

"The man's name is Angelos Nikakis and he is the mayor of Mikonos, that's a ..."

"I KNOW WHAT MYKONOS IS", roared the Emir. "I'll call the Greek president to arrest this sodomite!"

Mansoor almost laughed – just almost.

"Your Highness. The president would not have the right to do that. In Greece, there is no Emir who determines everything. And the mayors are elected by the people!"

"They've chosen a sodomite?", the Emir asked in disbelief.

"Yes, I think even with almost 90 percent. The man is popular and obviously very capable!"

"And has seduced my son!"

"I disagree. It was Khaled who readjusted this Nikakis and did not gave up. The mayor was already married!"

Now the Emir understood nothing anymore. "Married to a woman?"

No, you idiot. With a man, Mansoor thought. "No, with a man. But Khaled has probably twisted his way into Nikakis´ head. Then he left his husband!"

"An adulterer AND sodomite!"
No, a gay man who felt in love. Something normal. Mansoor sighed.
"We have to do something. I will not imagine what they think in Dubai and Abu Dhabi", the Emir complained.
"It would not be the first gay son of an Emir", Mansoor argued.
"I'm warning you. These were just malicious rumors from Tehran. I've been told that in Dubai and I do not doubt the words ... "
"Whatever. What should we do?"
"Get him home and then get him treated. There's definitely a method!"

Sweet naivety, how charming you are.
"That would be a kidnapping and would lead to a diplomatic scandal", Mansoor said.
"Maybe you can tell the other, this ..."
"Nikakis"
"Yes, offer money", suggested the Emir.
"That does not work. He's not interested in money and incorruptible after all I know!"
The Emir raised his eyebrows. It was not often that someone could resist a bundle of money.
'The two love each other. You can really see that on the photos!"
"PHOTOS?? Bring it on!"
That's exactly what Mansoor wanted to avoid, but he had no choice.
The Emir grimaced, but he had to admit that he had never seen Khaled so happy.

"Mansoor, that must end. Fast and forever!"
"As I said, there would be a scandal. By all respect, we would have to ask Dubai first",
"Mansoor contradicted.
"I have to do a damn shit. This is a family affair. And I'll handle it alone!"
Aha, Mansoor thought. We should take over the dirty work again.
"Kidnapping does not make sense. Nikakis would stage a media hype. And Khaled would do anything to return to Mikonos! "
"And if we neutralize this gay mayor?", the Emir asked.
Neutralize? It means murder, Mansoor thought.
"To Murder a Greek in Greece? You cannot mean that serious, he said.
The Emir became silent.
Mansoor already guessed what would come next.
"Then Khaled has to die. He's not my son anymore. And it would be the intended punishment, according to the holy book!"
And you raped your own niece, but the Sharia does not apply to the Emir. Mansoor sighed.
"Difficult. That too would be rippling!"
The Emir shook his head.
"Not if we do it skillfully. There must not be connections to us. Let's say that Tehran is behind it, because Khaled was in secret contact with the Israelis!"

"That was on your behalf!" Mansoor said indignantly.

"Right. But is history now. Well, Mansoor, we agree. Introduce the necessary steps. And I expect a success, is that clear?"

Mansoor was paralyzed, but he nodded.

"Before that, I will talk to Athens. Maybe it works with a little bit of pressure", the Emir said.

This will be a disgrace. Does he even know that the president is not the head of government at all? Anyway, both won´t believe what they will hear.

One thing Mansoor did not tell the Emir: that the Prime Minister and Nikakis are friends.

Mansoor left the palace and got into his car. "Fast. Into the flat!"

Because Raschid already waited. Mansoor was heartbroken at the thought of this sensational body.

I have to be careful that my head does not roll in the end – literally.

If the Emir knew that I slept with Khaled, he would have stoned me personally. Mainly because Khaled had just turned 17 at the time.

But it was Khaled who had come to him at that time, after it was clear by subtle hints that Khaled must be gay. Only this idiot did not realize ... You don´t see what you don´t want to know.

I should have restrained myself. But I could not. He was so hungry. Poor guy.

It happened only once. And Mansoor had kept Khaled's secret for years and made sure that from the various foreign trips no rumors reached Fudscheirah.
This Nikakis is a lucky guy.
But it will not last long.
Because my head is more important to me.

21

Mansoor, chief of the secret service of Fudscheira, relaxed in his chair. The night with Rashid was more than enjoyable. The little bastard has a lot of astonishing skills. Where the hell had he learned that?
Mansoor sighed. One week. One week he had to wait now, until he was allowed to touch this beautiful body again.
But I must be careful.
Yesterday, the little idiot started talking about a common future. Mansoor could not believe what he was hearing. You are 17 and I am 38. You are nothing and I am one of the most powerful men in the country, he thought.
It would not take long and Rashid would blackmail him. Maybe Mansoor would manage to settle the whole thing with money. Otherwise, Rashid would go the

same way as two of his predecessors. As a coyote food on the dump.

And now he had the problem Khaled in his neck. Couldn´t that idiot act in secret? No, it had to be the mayor of Mikonos. It was clear that it would become public. Mansoor had known about it for weeks. The pilot of the Crown Prince's machine was on his payroll and had taken pictures.

Mansoor could understand Khaled. This Nikakis was really a beauty. But Khaled should have known that the whole thing has no future. At first everything seemed to be harmless, because Nikakis did not want to leave his husband, but Khaled had persisted. He visited Mikonos - and thus Nikakis - again and again.

And managed to destroy the marriage of Nikakis. Mansoor knew about the charm and eloquence of Khaled.

Nikakis had moved out, Khaled immediately rushed to Mikonos and now they live together in Agios Ioannis at "Villas del Mar".

Mansoor already knew all this.

But what am I doing now?

Khaled would never come voluntarily.

For a kidnapping Mansoor would need at least five men and even then, it would be difficult to bring Khaled from the island. Especially not with a furious Angelos Nikakis in the neck, who as commissioner and mayor had all options and always uses them.

Therefore, the nickname "Emir" was correct.

No, it would only be the final solution.
A single action, clean - and without any traces.
Nikakis would know who was behind it, but he would not be able to prove it.
He googled Khaled and clicked on "Pictures."
He is even more beautiful than before. God, he was only seventeen then, so grateful that he finally knew where he belongs.
We only did it once. It was madness, but I just could not control myself.
The two are really a nice couple.
But my head is more important to me.
Mansoor had scruples - for about ten seconds.
Then he picked up the phone.

22

Meanwhile, Angelos and Khaled decided to stay in the sinkhole this day.
A few more hours to enjoy happiness. Before the eye of the hurricane would lie over them. And then it would start.
Sofianidis, the resort's director, came running. Nobody knew who the owners were. Some sort of hedge fund based in Jersey.
"I hope everything is to your satisfaction, Royal Highness and Mr. Mayor!"

"We really like it", Khaled said. "I would like to stay here forever. The view is fantastic. But my better half wants something simpler!"

"Maybe you can persuade the Emir, oh, sorry, the mayor!"

Angelos wanted to change the subject. Because the ideas about in what kind of house we will live are very different, he thought.

"Oh, Sofianidis, we have a problem!"

Only one? Sofianidis asked himself inwardly.

"We are happy to help!"

"Good. It will not be long before dozens of broadcast vans arrive!"

Sofianidis beamed. That would be the best advertisement ever.

"I do not want any of these hyenas to come near us", Angelos said firmly.

"Our staff is trained for that. We have a lot of exclusive guests who demand absolute discretion! I would make a statement that you are staying at our resort, but you want to stay undisturbed!"

"For my part, yes", Angelos said. "But what about drones?"

Sofianidis smiled.

"Yes. The times of paparazzi in the trees are probably over. Although we have no trees here!"

Sofianidis laughed about his own joke.

"It started two years ago with the first mini-drones. At that time, an English Royal was with us. At first, we did not know what to do.

We could not use anti-aircraft missiles, but now the technology is more discreet", said Sofianidis.

"And how does it work?" Angelos asked, interested in his job.

"Please follow me into the 'Defense center'." Angelos and Khaled followed Sofianidis into the middle section of the resort

"So, here we are. That box over there is the so-called tracker. It will detect the drones and trigger an alarm."

Then came a voice from the radio.

"Boss, there is an ERT car is arriving. With satellite dish! "

ERT – the Greek state television.

"Good that we're already here", Angelos said. "Then we can watch the system in action!"

And it took only five minutes until the tracker struck and the mini-drone was visible.

It flew in the direction of the pool area. Apparently, they wanted to film Angelos and Khalid holding hands on the sun lounger. Or better more.

"Now watch out", Sofianidis said.

He picked up a small box with a short antenna.

"A pity", he said.

Then a push on the button and the drone stopped in the air. Then it began to stumble and went into low altitude flight,

down to the rocks. The light on the jammer went out, indicating that the drone had finally landed. For the last time.

Angelos grinned.

"I will put that on my shopping list. Would you be so kind to shoot down the rest? Only today. Tomorrow we'll face the vultures! "

23

When Angelos and Khaled were back by the pool, Khaled took his phone and gave orders for two minutes. At least that's what it sounds like, Angelos thought. A "Schukran" – "thank you" in Arab did not appear in the text. I hope he never talks to me that way.

"Relax, sweetheart, you want to get away from here quickly. You feel uncomfortable in this luxury. So, I have instructed my two magnets to canvass the real estate agents and to make appointments for tomorrow. Only for normal properties, no luxury villas", Khaled said.

Angelos got up and sat on Khaled.

"Thank you. I want to lead a normal life. I hope you can handle it!"

"I get along with everything, the main thing is that you're on my side", Khaled answered.

"Heavens, your green eyes are a deadly weapon", Angelos said and smiled.

"And the second weapon shoots up if you continue slipping on me. Oh goodness!"

Of course, that was what Angelos was inciting.

"Ah, the royal scepter ..."

"... is about to burst. Grace", Khaled squeezed out.

Angelos redeemed Khaled.

"Where are your bodyguards actually?"

"In a hotel at the airport. I told them I am on a secret mission! "

Angelos laughed loudly.

"So, ascending the mayor is a secret mission? It was not very secret, as we now know!"

"The guys will get the order from Fudscheirah tomorrow to fly home anyway. Should we bet?", Khaled said.

You may be right, Angelos thought.

"Let's enjoy today. Tomorrow we have too much to do. In addition to the real estate agents, my yacht will arrive. Otherwise my dad will require it!"

Angelos laughed.

"Aha. So, a yacht belongs to our normal life? How modest!"

"Now. Just see it as a transport option. We do not need a plane to Athens and sometimes the Commissioner needs a boat for his investigation!"

Khaled smiled.

"This will be the most luxurious patrol boat in history. And with a blue light on the roof sure an eye-catcher", Angelos said.

Angelos' cell phone growled.

"Heavens", he said.

"Giorgios. The town hall. I must answer. Excuse me!"

"Alright!"

"Giorgios, what's up?"

A question whose answer Angelos could already foresee.

"Emir, hell is going on here. Everybody ... "

"... TV stations called, plus ten newspapers, right?"

"That's the understatement of the year", Giorgios replied.

'There will be a message tomorrow at 10 o'clock on our Facebook page. There will be no interviews. After all, that's my private business!"

"Uh, yes. So, it's true? You marry the prince?" Giorgios shot in the dark.

"Giorgios, I'm still married to Alex. But it could be. Someday!"

Khaled smiled gratefully.

"Oh, there is something else. A colleague of the archaeologist called. She has some information. But she just wants to talk to you!", Giorgios said.

And Angelos got a guilty conscience.

The murder case. Heavens. I totally forgot it because of being in love.

Great Commissioner.

"Ask her if she can be at 'Burro' by twelve!"

"Alright, Emir. And have fun today", Giorgios said smugly.

"Dumbass!"

Angelos turned left to Khaled and shrugged.

"Alright, sweetheart. It's your job and I knew that before. So tomorrow we have a press release, look for a house, a hearing and picking up the yacht. I can only stand it if you spoil me tonight", Khaled said with a smile.
"I am at your service, Your Royal Highness!"
"Naughty guy!"

24

Adam Resniak was lying in his sun-chair behind the house, satisfied with himself. Everything went as planned. He had quickly settled in Mikonos and found out that he liked it here.

He had mastered his first assignment brilliantly.

His decision to accept only orders from his "old" agency had been correct. One of the others had tried to kill him. The risk that it had been his original agency, which ordered his death, was low.

His last orders, including the failed, came from other intermedia. So, he stayed well clear of them.

He remained in the "Cycladic sinking", except for his regular employer.

Of course, he knew that the first assignment after his escape was a kind of rehearsal. The pay was far below the norm, but Resniak could understand it. They wanted to test whether he was still the "old Resniak" and whether he still had the qualities that had made him one of the top earners in his business segment.

The assignment was harmless and caused him no problem. The person was neutralized without leaving a trace. He was satisfied with him.

Now, today came the second order. To his great astonishment the site will also be Mikonos. Hard to believe. The island is obviously not just a sleepy rock.

The fee was one of the highest ever offered. He did not know that his agency offers such delicate jobs. He always thought that they were focused on cases below the media threshold, not to make the "big players" angry. He felt his nervousness in his own body. A kick, which he missed for years. A challenge.

But what arrived today, encrypted via a server in Dagestan, amazed him.

That certainly does not fall into the category of "murders that do not interest anyone!".

Well, the fee was also very high, and he could live well for half a year. Or even longer. After 30 minutes of reflection, he agreed. It would not be easy. He would have to do it without the head shot from a quiet position. Wouldn´t work. The deadly shots I have to make from a moving vehicle, Resniak assumed. Too many imponderables in the equation, he thought first. But then he thought of the fee and agreed.

More detailed information would arrive soon via email. Of course, Resniak knew the victim. Not a real celebrity, but ...

You've done that dozens of times: out of the car, from the bike and your hand was still steady, so what are you worried about?

Just a question of good planning. Resniak had always rejected quick orders. I always want to know everything, check myself and then decide, even if it takes two weeks. Professional killer and hurry in his opinion are two words that definitely do not match.

25

Although the two lovers did not leave their place by the pool, there was no peace. Again, the mobile grumbled.

"The Prime Minister", moaned Angelos.

"He's calling you? You seem to have more influence than I thought", Khaled said.

Angelos laughed.

"Nonsense. We only know each other. I think he's a crook. Like all politicians!"

"Are not you one, too?"

Angelos innocent look followed.

"I am the famous exception!"

Khaled laughed.

"Don´t you want to call the 'rogue' back?"

"Only at a stretch. Let´s get it over! "

It was not long before he had Villa Maximos on the line.

"Can you keep your pants on at some point?", an annoyed Migiakis growled.

"Envious?" Angelos asked back.

"Not really. Couldn´t you have grabbed a tourist? Did it necessarily have to be a Crown Prince? "

"Who sent him here?"

"I did. But I could not have guessed that you were puzzling the poor guy!"

'The 'poor guy' wanted me, not the other way around. And he lies next to me and can confirm it to you. Are you calling to inquire about my sex life? You don´t have other things to do?"

"Listen. Seriously. The Ambassador was here before and seriously demanded to lock you up. Although I would do so with pleasure, he was astonished that I cannot. Where do these desert sons live? On the moon?"

"Shall I hand the phone over to one of the desert sons?"

The conversation became increasingly funny for Angelos.

"Seriously, Angelos. Pay attention. Things are rocketing, and customs are harsh in the Middle East. And please take this warning seriously!"

That was a different sound than before.

"Good, Antonis. I understood the warning. But it could still be that I marry Khaled!"

"For heaven´s sake", was Migiakis' last comment.

"Goofy," Angelos said, tossing the phone in the meadow.

But after another hour, Angelos became restless. He shifted on his couch and growled to himself.

"What is, my beauty?", Khaled asked.

"I am not made for the pool or the beach. I cannot just lie around. I'm so sorry. You fell in love with someone who is full of quirks", Angelos replied.

Khaled smiled.

"Come along!"

He took Angelos by the hand and led him around the corner of the villa. There was a bed with a raised back.

"Again?", Angelos asked, astonished.

"No. Just lie down! "

What Angelos did.

Khaled lay down next to him and laid his hand on Angelos´ heart. Or more precisely: on the skin over the heart. Gently, he began to stroke and massage the place.

"What are you doing there?"

"That's what mothers do in Arabia when their children are upset or scared. Just close your eyes", Khaled said softly.

And in fact, it took only a minute for Angelos to come to great peace. The need to do something was swept away.

"Sorcerer?", Angelos asked, about to purr like a kitten.

"You can call me Aladdin!"

After a short break, Khaled said.

"After the rape you escaped from yourself and your memories. How everyone would do it. But you don´t have to anymore. You are no longer looking. You have arrived. I am your final destination!"

And as in love as Khaled looked at him, Angelos had no more doubts.

"Maybe you are right!"

Unfortunately, the caressing had another effect.

"Aladdin had an ulterior motive", Angelos said with a grin.

"I am innocent. But if Mr. Mayor pulls out his magic wand ... "

"... the rabbit should flee!"

It took three espressos to get Angelos´ spirits back.

"I have a monster as husband!"

Khaled beamed.

"Did you just say 'husband'? The monster would like to marry you!"

'That already went wrong once. And you should wait until you know me better. Maybe you'll lose your appetite soon?"

"No way. As I said, you have arrived. I'm your target and you're mine", Khaled said firmly.

"Well and there can´t be one who is more beautiful and smarter than you!"

"You're absolutely right!", Angelos replied and laughed.
"One more thing: I have a request and I do not want you to ask why!"
"So, you mean an order of the Emir?", Khaled asked with a smile.
"Yes. Not negotiable. Just trust me", Angelos replied.
"My trust in you is limitless. So, what does my Lord and Master want? "
And Angelos told him.

26

You don't mean that serious. I need an e-scooter from the bedroom to the kitchen", Angelos growled when they visited the second house. Already the first one felt into the category "nouveau-riche-villa". Exactly what Angelos did not want. And the second was so oversized that even the land consumption made the mayor Angelos Nikakis angry.

"Sorry, my lackeys had probably thought of a palace when they heard 'house'. How about we go with them to a normal house. So that I and they understand what you mean. Then we can search for new objects.

It's only a bit rushing, because I expect their dismissal every minute. After all, I am no longer a Crown Prince and frankly, I do not want to have people around me – except you! "

"But I stay with 'My Prince'. I already got used to it. Even if you are only my prince", Angelos answered.

"That's exactly what I wanted!"

"Honestly, I want a house like ours, so - sorry ..."

"Already understood. The house of you and Alex. Come on, let's go there so the two see it too. Then they cannot go wrong", Khaled said.

Angelos hesitated.

"Do not worry, we do not go in, just outside. I have only one request: I need a small pool - and you'll like it", Khaled said.

"You decide, because I cannot contribute much. I cannot sell the house in Ornos. I do not want to do that to Alex", Angelos replied.

'That honors you. But it will be our common house, half of it is yours. After all, you're a permanent guest. Aren´t you?", Khaled asked softly.

Angelos rolled his eyes.

"Why do you doubt me?"

'The fear you'll get tired of me", Khaled said softly.

"You wanted me and now you have me - until your death. Which has just been postponed", Angelos added.

Khaled beamed and Angelos kissed him passionately.

"Now let's go. I have to go to the interrogation at twelve", Angelos said.

27

A ngelos turned left to the parking lot in front of the 'Burro', which was located on the ring road, very popular with the Greeks. And as always, the idiots parked crisscross.

He entered the bar and a young woman waved to him. She had told Giorgios that she knew Angelos.

"Yassas, Mrs. Petritsis!"

"Irini is enough, Mr. Mayor!"

"Then Angelos will do. One moment please!"

Angelos got up and said aloud:

"First, you'll park like normal people in the future, or I'll come tomorrow with a bucket of white paint. Second, the prince is doing well and, thirdly, tomorrow we are buying a house together. Now you have something to chatter! "

Angelos sat down again.

Irini laughed.

"You speak straightforward. Shall I not call you 'Emir?'"

"No, but you should always take control about rumors yourself. This increases the true content! But we are not here for that. You wanted to tell me something about the archaeologist."

Antonis Kyriakos. Embarrassing. I almost did not remember the name. All because of the Khaled confusion.

"Yes. It's just awful. He was such a nice colleague", Petritsis said sadly.

"You had a relationship with him?", Angelos asked, adding, "sorry, if I ask so directly!"

Irini looked perplexed.

"The subtle way is not yours, or?"

"That saves my and your time, Irini!"

She sighed.

"Yes, we were together. For six months. We got to know each other on Delos. For archaeologists there is probably no better place to fall in love. It was really magical!"

Tears came to her.

Angelos rummaged for a handkerchief.

"Do not worry, not used!"

It took half a minute for Irini to take a deep breath.

"We were really happy. But without bigger plans. He was married and had children. This terrible person! A witch. Have you had the pleasure?"

Angelos nodded.

"I had. You should kill her and someday someone will do. The man must have suffered. I always wonder why there are women's shelters but no men's houses. The emancipation is still far behind!"

Irini laughed.

"If there were more women like Antonis´ shrew, then I would donate to a men's house!"

"There are plenty of awful women", Angelos said, who, as a "male gay", had nothing feminine about him and he had a problem when gay men behave like women. It´s each person´s own decision, but tolerance does not mean that you must like something. This fundamentally disturbed view on female affairs also led to a suspicious attitude towards women. As commissioner, he found that women are less brutal but more insidious. And in the first place, he could not find anything erotic about the female body.

"How do heterosexuals get an erection?", he asked Alex once, because Alex was married to a woman.

"I forgot it", was the answer.

He had missed the first half of Irini's sentence by his rambling thoughts.

"... happy if he was here again."

"Good. You were together. But what does this have to do with the murder? Unless you want to confess, which would be fine", Angelos said, but smiled.

"I have to disappoint you. I would assume his wife, but she's too stupid to build a bomb. But I have a guess what could be the reason for the murder!"

"Well, that would help me", Angelos said with a smile.

"Do you know what a 'Dareikos' is?", Irini asked.

"Sounds Persian", Angelos said.

"Goud guess. You are right. A 'Dareikos' is a golden coin from the time of the Persian King Xerxes, around 480 BC!"

"Those were the first coins at all, right?", Angelos asked.

"Yes. The Persian king wanted to eliminate the confusion in the trade and the constant frauds. So, he had introduced coins: the 'Dareikos' made of gold and the 'Siglos' in silver", Irini explained.

"So, they are extremely valuable?", Angelos asked.

Irini shook her head slightly.

'That's such a thing. Archaeological no, because there are enough of them. A trove is no longer a sensation. But a 'Dareikos' costs around 2.000 Euros! The 'Siglos' around 700 €."

"Therefore, Antonis found coins on Delos, but kept them to himself", Angelos guessed.

"For us. He wanted to raise enough money so we could start a new life after his divorce. Even with the two salaries as archaeologists, that would not be possible!"

Always the same story: the crisis as a justification for theft and crime, Angelos thought.

"However, he did not tell me any details", Irini added quickly.

"Because you did not want to know. Then you feel more innocent", Angelos replied.

"If he found these coins on Delos, why have not they been discovered long ago? No archaeological site has been digged up so often. They should have found them sooner!"

"Not necessarily. First, archaeologists are specialized idiots. I am an expert on scrolls, writing material and papyrus. But I have not the slightest idea about coins. But more important is the second point: the coins do not look like coins at first sight. They are not flat like today, but oval in length and height!"

"Like little pebbles?" Angelos asked.

"That is almost right. They are difficult to find if soiled!"

"About what amount are we talking about? For 100,000 euros he would have to find 50 pieces!"

"I have no idea. I remained on the sidelines as far as possible. He probably also wanted to protect me", Irini said.

"So, you do not know to whom he sold the coins?", Angelos asked.

Irini shook her head.

Angelos had not expected anything else either.

But one thing was clear to him: Antonis' brother worked in the Ministry of Culture and was responsible for exportation certificates. I will eat my hat if his brother is not a link of this chain. Or better: was, because the 'link Antonis' consists now of 45 individual parts. But he did not get any further in his thoughts, because the mobile grumbled. Alex. Cursed.

28

If he could come over, Alex asked. Angelos wanted to avoid this in the first days of separation. Too fresh to settle things in peace. Besides, I only have about an hour, then I must pick up Khaled from the harbor, he thought.

He sighed, but then he drove down to Ornos. Goose bumps hit him, because Angelos had not yet checked off the breakup. It happened just 72 hours ago.

Alex stood already in the door. He smiled, but his face did not match.

"May I kiss you on the cheek without being stoned by the prince?", he asked.

"You can even hug me. And his name is Khaled", Angelos answered.

The hug was a little too tight, Angelos thought.

"Listen, Alex. I think it's way too early to discuss details. I want to do it all without a fight!"

"'To discuss details' sounds like it did not mean anything!"

"You know that's not true. I was a good partner and husband to you. I have never cheated on you and have always been honest. The latter was perhaps the mistake!" Alex nodded.

"You have been and remain the love of my life. But I do not want to burden you. You have decided differently, and I wish you good luck. I'll have to manage it alone!" That was the real Alex.

"Maybe everything would have gone differently if you had lied to me about Khaled. I wouldn´t have known anything and maybe ..."

"... the Khaled affair would not or will not work. That´s what you wanted to say, or? You should know me. I do not do things by halves. No future for you and your hairy neighbor?" Angelos could not resist.

"That was just ... I do not know what that was. A misfire. In revenge. The most serious blackout of my life", Alex said sadly.

"Can we still be friends? And you try to accept my new relationship with Khaled?"

"The bad thing is that I like him. And I can understand you. He is charming and looks perfect. I only curse the day you met him. Not him!"

"And I thank God for this day," Angelos replied.

"Probably Allah", Alex said smiling.

"No, I have not yet converted. I do not like religion, and you know that! "

"It was just a joke. Espresso?"

"Yes, a quick one. I must pick up Khaled at the harbor. "

"I can take you there. I would like to say 'hello'. I do not want to be the ex in the background. If he opposes, that does not work with our friendship. What are we doing with all this stuff here?"

The stuff was all the computers and monitors for policing. The placement in the kitchen in the commissioner´s home made sense - when they were still living together.

"We leave it here. I am the mayor and you become the sole commissioner. Or get Giorgios. In severe cases, I can join you if you wish", Angelos said.

"You have much more experience of felony than me. You've solved all the cases! "

"Not all. But we have to clarify that at the next murder. Or, of course, better before. But: we don´t have a murder every month!"

The "before the next murder" should be a shorter time span than Angelos thought.

It was just an hour. No, less.

29

Gas! ", shouted Angelos.

Alex had slowed down automatically and already opened the door.
The situation in which two souls wrestle inside a policeman:

Help the victim.

Track the offender.

And Angelos opted for the latter. Alex was used to following Angelos' decisions, so he let go.

But Alex was confused. Khaled, Angelos' great love lay in front of the harbor building, badly injured or dead.

You must be an extremely cold-blooded person to not worry about the victim first. But cold-blooded or heartless? That was certainly not Angelos.

"You do not want ...?", Alex began.

"DON´T LOSE HIM", Angelos shouted.

They were lucky. At the exit of the port, two trucks blocked the road. The bike had to brake sharply and avoided by the sidewalk. Three hundred yards further, the assassin again had a problem. A delivery van, which had supplied a supermarket, pushed backwards out of the exit, regardless of the traffic.

Angelos could have cheered. Long live the Greek driving style!

The bike had to brake sharply and almost came to a stop before it could pass the truck on the left.

And so, Alex and Angelos were back in the race.

The assassin gave full throttle and turned half left to the bypass-road. Free track, because the road was wide. The rock walls threw back the loud roar of the motorcycle. But the SUV could easily follow him.

I'll take everything back, thought Alex, who had protested violently against the purchase. Too pretentious and too wide for parking. The completely wrong car for Mikonos. With a Peugeot you cannot track anyone, and besides, our roads are so bad that they are actually terrain, Angelos argued.

Moreover, it was not a private car, but a police vehicle.

That's the only reason why they had a chance and were only fifty yards behind the bike when they reached the plateau and approached the first roundabout.

"Left past the traffic island", Angelos shouted. In fact, the motorcycle turned left and did not care about the roundabout.

How did he know that ...?

"Straight line. Look, he wants to outpace us. Full throttle", shouted Angelos.

Right. Go straight for two kilometers. Perfect for a motorcycle.

People on the right and left of the road towards Ano Mera ripped apart. The people at the zebra crossing also registered the danger and remained paralyzed. The right decision. The assassin rushed in front of them, the SUV passed behind them.

The distance became bigger.

Suddenly Angelos looked at the display, Alex, registered but had to continue focusing on driving. He believed to have understood "thank God".

"That guy's good", Alex yelled.

"That's his job," Angelos yelled back.

Continue for 500 meters until you reach the 180 degrees-bend to the right. An advantage for the bike, unless a tourist from Paradise wants to get back to the hotel. The small road ends exactly at the apex of the curve. Please, let there be a jerk from the beach, Angelos thought.

But it did not need a tourist.

30

Giorgios Menos has been working for twenty years at the gas station near to the bend. As a gas station attendant, because self-fueling is not common in Greece. Where else should the 100,000 men work?

He was already 67 and still had to work. Living on a pension was simply not possible. Forty percent cut in the last five years.

And as usual with older men, Giorgios´ prostate was just a malfunctioning machine anymore.

The toilet in the gas station was a roughly 80 meters away. It was closer when you walked across the street to pee, which Giorgios regularly did.

He looked to the left - nothing.

He looked to the right - a scooter, far away. He did not think about a motorbike because the roads on Mikonos do not match with a two-wheeler which is fast as an arrow.

Giorgios had just taken his second step, as he noticed out of the corner of his eye that the scooter, which was not one, was just twenty yards away.

He jumped forward. His bad luck: The motorcyclist decided to drive past the obstacle on the right.

One hundredth of a second later Giorgios, the man in black and his motorcycle hurtled through the air.

Giorgios up, the assassin and the motorcycle over the boundary wall into the small canyon behind.

"Hit", shouted Angelos and Alex braked hard. "You to the pedestrian", ordered Angelos. Because I must get this bastard - if he has survived the fall. But human scum has the disappointing habit of being tough, he thought.

Angelos ran to the small wall and looked down.

Ten meters of flat terrain and then it goes down into the gorge. He must have landed in it, because otherwise I would see him on the field above, Angelos thought. On the one hand, he was relieved, because there is still a chance that the assassin lives.
Dead he would have no use.
Angelos Nikakis could have calmed down - the culprit was still alive.

31

A dam Resniak hung in a bush just below the edge. It was not a deep gorge, but the cut of an earlier creek that had capitulated to the heat 50 years ago. Below him were only three meters, not steep and with some of this scrub. A crash would not be dangerous, but you would hear it. From above he could hear the policemen talking. They were less than twenty yards away.
Mission successfully completed, he thought, then immediately laughed inside. I could be dead and if they find me, it was my last job. And I'm worried about the customer review. I was unlucky. Wrecked trucks, an idiot just driving backwards and an old fool walking across the street. You cannot plan that. However, I underestimated the motorization

of the local police. Where the hell did, they get SUVs from empty cash registers? Well, the dossier said that the friend of the victim was the local commissioner and that he should not be underestimated. Well, I already knew that. The personal relation certainly motivated the Commissioner to stick to me like this.

Well, the job was done. The Commissioner is solo again, because of two perfect hits in Khaled´s chest: target dead.

Adam Resniak was surprised that he had weathered the fall well at first sight.

Amazingly good when you think of the threefold collision - with the old fool, the parapet and then the rock - or, thankfully, the bush on the rock.

He carefully moved every major muscle and toes and fingers. Sure, the whole body hurts, how could it have been different.

I must leave here. As fast and silent as possible.

It would not take long for the police to reach the gorge. He only had an extra timeframe because they rightly suspected that he still had his weapon. Nevertheless: away from here was the motto.

He moved with the utmost care, of course in pain, but that was certainly more bearable than twenty years of jail.

Adam Resniak reached the bottom of the gorge and took a deep breath. Now, down or up? It would be more logical and

convenient to walk to the end of the valley. So, I walk in the opposite direction. With the injuries difficult, but the profile of the professional killer includes physical fitness as a prerequisite - and Resniak was extremely fit even though he was already forty-four.
He expected to hear the rattle of a helicopter at any moment, and there was no coverage in this area.
Except for a few shrubs. The black clothes are not much help either.
He tormented himself uphill, then disappeared behind the ridge. Discarded the pants and jacket there and continued to run only with the jeans.
Nice and slow like a tourist. And then on side roads. The helmet had saved his life and prevented him from getting facial scratches. He would have noticed. Adam Resniak reached the small road behind the ridge and tried to walk as normal and upright as possible. He was extra fortunate, because in front of him ran a group of four raucous tourists who obviously wanted to walk to Paradise Beach to save the bus fee.
He kept the distance so that it looked like he had fallen behind in this group.
Not thirty seconds later he heard the rattle of the helicopter. He let the distance to the group getting smaller and hoped that due to the speed, the pilot would not notice that he is slightly limping. The raucous noise of the

helicopter came closer, but then it flew to the left to the airport.

Adam Resniak exhaled.

Walk for another five kilometers and then I'm at home. I do not need to inform the client. The positive message he will get by the Internet or on TV.

And Resniak was right. Although Angelos wanted to jump over the wall to look for the assassin, Alex pulled him back.

"He still has his weapon, my God!"

"And where are ours? One should be in the car", Angelos said.

Alex hemmed and hawed.

"Uh, no. I cleaned it yesterday and forgot to put it back in the car!"

Angelos got a bright red head.

'Thought again about hairy neighbor? Should I use the jack as a weapon?"

"That was mean. I have made a mistake!"

"Not your first," Angelos muttered.

'Then call the helicopter, but until it comes the culprit is gone!"

It was 3 pm. Currently, the two flights from Munich approach and then the helicopter gets no take-off. Cursed.

32

With every meter that they came closer to the clinic, Angelos became more nervous. Alex had not even stopped when Angelos jumped out of the car.

That can only be love, Alex thought with a sigh.

To whom could I vent my anger on? Only to me. I had it in my hands. How could I? Yes, I was hurt, but that was a feeling that had taken possession of me for a few days – and I should have endured it. Every marriage has its crises. And now?

Meanwhile, Angelos crashed into the room of Medical Director André.

"Is he alright?", Angelos exclaimed.

André smiled and nodded.

Angelos grabbed him by both sides of his head and kissed him on the mouth.

"I'm immune", he said with a grin.

"Should I send Alex in?", Angelos asked cheekily.

"Why not? He's cured now", André joked.

"He cheated me. But that's water under the bridge. Honestly, I could imagine you will be a nice couple. And you will hardly believe it: despite your dislike of me, I think it would be a good solution!", Angelos said.

"Now the Emir works as matchmaker, too. This island degenerates under this mayor. But now go to your prince. Room 6!"

Angelos stormed the two rooms further and teared open the door.

Khaled.

He smiled.

"Puuuuh", Angelos exhaled. "I was pretty sure, but ..."

Khaled raised an eyebrow.

"After your next clue that someone will shoot on me, maybe you should tell me first!"

Angelos smiled.

"How come? And seriously, it was just a gut feeling and this strange remark by Migiakis. Therefore, my request to wear the protection vest the next days, including the arm and leg protection!"

"Aha, that's why I should wear the kandura. Under normal clothes that wouldn´t have fit! "

Kandura. What is commonly known as the 'sheikh costume' is cut extremely wide.

"And if he would have hit my head?", Khaled growled.

"That was completely out of the question. Not from a vehicle. And for a shot with a scoped rifle, it takes two things: a location without people - on Mikonos the chance is nil. On the plateau too many people and high roofs do not exist around the harbor.

But more important: the wind. Professional killers can consider the wind, but no gusts. And the assassin had heard the same weather report as I did: 3 to 5 Bofors, with gusts up to 70. So, this option was excluded! "

"YOU BANKED ON THE WEATHER REPORT?"

"Khaled. It has to be like that. Now the client and the assassin believe that you are dead. I already have the first sympathy-SMS on the phone!"

Angelos laughed.

'This gives us the time to track the gentlemen and then take care of them!"

Khaled nodded.

"Who do you think is behind it?"

"You've already answered the question yourself", Angelos said.

Khaled nodded.

"My father!"

Angelos nodded.

'The ambassador must have hinted, otherwise Migiakis would not have warned me to watch out!"

"Couldn´t the Prime Minister have said clearly that they would try to assassinate me?", Khaled growled.

"Politicians do not do that!"

"You're one yourself", Khaled replied.

"I am different. And nicer", Angelos said.

Khaled laughed loudly.

"Please stay so modest. Now come and kiss me finally!"

"With the greatest pleasure!"

Angelos sat down on the edge of the bed.

"Are the pains endurable?", he asked, because vests prevent bullets from entering the body, but the force of the impact can still break ribs.

"I´m gonna make it. According to André just bruises, but they'll be big!"

'Then we should test the vital signs!"

Angelos grinned, put his hand under the blanket and put it on Khaled's leg.

"Hm. So, obviously there is no harm here. Four seconds", Angelos said, laughing aloud.

"But I should first ask André if oral therapy is not too much for your blood pressure!"

"YOU WANT TO LET ME LIE HERE LIKE THIS? YOU ARE A SADIST!", Khaled squeezed out.

"No. I love my prince", Angelos said and his head disappeared under the covers.

"Good Lord", stammered Khaled.

Therapy was suddenly stopped after ten seconds. The Director stood in the door.

Khaled blushed while Angelos was still busy.

"Ah, the mayor and his favorite pastime", André mocked.

Only then did Angelos come out from under the blanket.

"It's only for his recovery", Angelos smirked.

"He has a severe post-traumatic disorder that is best treated orally. The trauma will be blown away, so to speak! "

"Aha. Would you like to treat the other male patients as well?", André etched.

"Oh no, I'll leave that to you!"

Khaled could hardly hold back anymore.

And André went red in the face.

"Well. I can control myself. I do not have to go to work in a hospital!"

André shouldn´t have said it.

"Well, then Alex will have very boring sex in the future", Angelos replied.

That was enough for André. He slammed the door.

Khaled laughed loudly.

Nobody can really keep up with your mouth! ", followed by Angelos' famous innocent look.

"Which mouth do you mean? The one under the blanket?"

"Both, my sweetheart!"

"Should I continue, your Royal Highness?" Angelos asked mischievously.

"Yes, slave, he may continue! Could I have that twice a day, please?"

Angelos shook his head.

"No way. Then the mayor gets a lockjaw. He is just too ... "

"Fine?", Khaled suggested.

"Nice and big. Let's put it this way!", Angelos answered.

33

While Khaled was in the seventh heaven, Nikos Kyriakos had already reached the floor above. A bullet had caused a cerebral disorder - the last of his life.

Unlike his brother, he was relatively well preserved, at least the body was a whole. He had always feared it but repressed his sorrows. Anyone who gets involved with these people will be eliminated early. Because confidants trigger a kind of migraine in the criminal´s head, which only disappears by meeting a bullet from a Glock or Beretta. And so, the former partner - and confidant - got his final migraine. He knew it when he opened the door. Nikos had no weapon in front of his face, but the guy looked like death. Three seconds later, Nikos flew down the hall. His wife broke up immediately. She could have called the police too, but that would be an exaggeration, she decided. Besides, she wanted to continue living, preferably without her husband. In this respect, she put in the visit a certain expectation.

And the rough Romanian tried his best. First, he strucked Nikos until he was just a whimpering thing.

"I forgot to introduce myself. How embarrassing. I am an employee of Mr. Mitrescu. You remember him?"

As if he would ever forget this day. It was the promise of a better life. He had the premonition that it would also ruin everything that evening, but greed was overriding fear. They murdered my brother first, and now it's my turn, Nikos thought. This coincided with the plans of Mr. Mitrescu's envoy. But: before the long journey, the Lord would still have a few tiny questions. The answers would not cause any problems for Nikos.

"The last delivery has failed. They did not like that in Bucharest! "

To put it mildly. The consequence was the decision to beam his brother Antonis into a very different time than just in the Delos time, 1500 years before the Lord, to whom Antonis came much closer than he had ever intended. To make an example.

But contrary to expectations, Nikos was unimpressed, at least this was the impression in Bucharest. The Romanian traders could not know that he had not got the last delivery of coins.

That stupid asshole had kept the last twenty coins and wanted to sell them to dealers one by one. For building a future. For himself and Irini.

It was madness and Nikos had told Antonis so.

You cannot end such a business relationship unilaterally and certainly not by mutual agreement. Unless one agrees with his own death.

The only problem was that Nikos' visitor did not want to believe the true facts.

"He didn´t bring anything during the last visit. I swear!"

The words came from a mouth that had lost much of its teeth. But that should have been just the prelude.

"That's not a good answer!"

The visitor pulled out a nail gun and Nikos was close to fainting.

"Believe me! He had nothing!"

That was not a good answer too.

Ten seconds later, Nikos had a nail in his left forearm. The visitor had previously pushed a pillow over Nikos face, the cry was still clearly heard. Two rooms further Nikos' wife had just one thought: am I the next? Her husband did not interest her.

She could have calmed down, because the visitor was fully focused on Nikos and trying to finally get the right answer.

But the second and third nail brought no new knowledge. Slowly the visitor realized that Nikos really did not know anything.

And that was not very forward-looking, because the visitor shot the useless Nikos in the head.

The visitor was not satisfied because the bearer of the message ...

At least one confidant was eliminated. However, he underestimated the pathological curiosity of women. And especially this one.

If the police will find Nikos, I'm automatically suspicious. In 90 percent of the murders, the perpetrator is one of the friends or the own family - and often the wife. In addition, I said to not only a few friends, Nikos should go to hell.

She ran to the balcony and looked down the street.

There he was. She pulled out her cell phone at lightning speed.

The Romanian crossed the street and looked left - back. Click.

No top shot, but a face she could deliver. Relief spread.

Double luck: the photo and: finally, I'm rid of this idiot Nikos.

34

Angelos and Khaled passed the checks in front of the "Villas de Mar". Hardly stopped, director Sofianidis came running.

"Mayor! Royal Highness. I hope you are doing well. I heard about an assassination. Some have said you are dead, Royal Highness!"

"We are not. Isn´t that obvious?", Angelos answered and took the director aside.

"Listen, it's important that you do not deny the message. Khaled is dead!"

"But he is there!"

Holy smoke, Angelos thought.

"Yes, but nobody should know, at least not too early. That's why no one will be allowed to enter our villa. A cleaner, but one that does not speak Greek or English. Maybe one that is not too intelligent", Angelos said.

The director finally seemed to understand.

"But then we cannot keep the standard anymore!"

"Do not worry. We can make a pizza ourselves!"

Hearing the word "pizza" the director made a face as if it were feces.

"As you wish, Mr. Mayor!"

"And no calls. If you have something urgent, slip a note under the door. Personally!"

"The wishes of our guests ..."

"Your biggest concern, I know", Angelos interrupted.

He went back to Khaled. Together they entered "their" villa.

Khaled gave Angelos a note.

"Five days bed rest? You miserable crook. You have turned your eyes on André just to get this medical report. You want to stay here if possible. And five days of permanent sex", Angelos said, but smiled.

Khaled looked innocent.

"But, honey, I was shot!"

"But you were not hit, and all parts still work!"

"We should check that again", Khaled said.

"No way. We did an hour ago. I'm not a machine", Angelos replied.

Two minutes later, they were sitting on the terrace.

Angelos' mobile grunted, but Khaled thought it was his.

"Khaled Nikakis. Oh, hello Alex. I think I got the wrong phone. Moment!"

Angelos growled.

"How many Nikakis would you like to have on the island? Now we are already three! Marriage proposal after just three days?", Alex said reproachfully.

"Nonsense. Khaled was joking. We are still married. No reason to worry.

Besides, I do not know what name you'll have after the divorce!"

Alex sighed.

"I leave it that way. It reminds me of my biggest mistake!"

'That you married me? Thank you for the flowers!"

"Nonsense. That I forgave you. Well. Life goes on somehow, although I do not know how. But that's not why I'm calling. I thought that the cameras from the scene show nothing effective because of the helmet. But the culprit will have left only a few minutes before. Maximum 15 minutes if he lives or stays in Kalafati. And when he got on the bike, he certainly did not have a helmet on. Or at least when leaving the house or hotel. That would be too noticeable. Maybe I'm lucky!"

Angelos was amazed. So much commitment on Alex's side?

"Yes, that sounds good, but it is a pagan work. Shall I come over and help?"

"No. Stay with Mr. Nikakis 3!"

"Alex, please!"

"It was a joke. I'll start now. I'll contact you! "

"I'm impressed," Angelos said to Khaled after the conversation ended.

"Maybe we can stay friends!"

"As long as he understands that you're mine now", Khaled answered.

"I'm not yours," Angelos said, smiling.

"Sweetie, my English is just nearly perfect and my Greek lousy. But that's really a strange language! "

"Aha. Wrong sentences, you will always put it on the language. You can forget that right away", Angelos said.

"Well then we speak Arabic", Khaled suggested.

"Touché, my prince!"

And again, the mobile grumbled.

"PM," Angelos said, rolling his eyes.

"Are you okay?", asked Migiakis, Prime Minister.

"Yes. Thanks to your warning, even if you could have been a bit clearer", Angelos said.

"Politicians are never clear!"

"I always thought you would be glad if I pass over the Jordan", Angelos growled.

"What do you think? You are my favorite mayor. You're terribly annoying, but you're the only one who says 'idiot' or 'goofy' to me. And I need that!" Migiakis laughed.

"But listen. I do not think it's all over yet. Arabs are vengeful. To your information: there are two Israelis surround you and there are also two of our agents coming!"

"Four men to protect a gay couple? Very progressive!"

"I am the head of progress, my dear Angelos!"

And Mr. Mayor got a laugh attack.

35

Only half an hour later, the phone vibrated again.

"I hope you turn it off at least during the wedding", Khaled said with a chuckle.

"What wedding?"

And Khaled threw his pillow towards Angelos. He laughed and wiped over his smartphone. Alex.

"I GOT IT. He RENTED the bike. At Hertz. I have camera shots without a helmet, but the guy is still hard to spot. Baseball cap, scarf and sunglasses!"

"I could kiss you!"

"That is forbidden by your prince, ain´t it?"

"Khaled, may I still kiss Alex?"

"On the cheek. Without tongue. Once a month!"

Khaled grinned.

"I'll send the shot to your phone", Alex said and hung up.

Angelos looked at the video and came up with an idea. He called his friend Nikos from the EYP, the Greek secret service.

"Nikos? Yes, we're fine. You must help me. I send you recordings and please check them with the face recognition! "

"I will!"

"The pictures do not reveal much!"

"You are underestimating our possibilities. The program is simply awesome! By the way, you will always be followed by two vehicles. We and the Israelis!"

"Why the Israelis? They guard an Arabian. Something new!", Angelos said confused.

"Your prince is apparently an important number. Lieutenant Colonel of the army. Three years in Sandhurst. Besides, he was involved in secret negotiations!"

Angelos sent the file.

"Are you alright, Lieutenant Colonel?", he asked Khaled who was grinning.

"I told you, I was not a spoiled prince. That can be of use to you. I can shoot like a professional killer!"

"Anything your future husband should know?"

"I did not think it was important. Excuse me. It was not the right time yet!"

"I do not have to stand at attention in front of you, do I?", Angelos asked.

"Only a part of you has to stand!"

"On command?"

"Oh no. That worked automatically so far. And usually in two seconds", Khaled said, smiling.

36

And? Is my general satisfied? At least for the next two hours? ", a sweaty Angelos asked.

Khaled, too, was completely exhausted.

"Good lord. The monster is you, not me!"

"A complaint?"

Khaled rolled over to Angelos and looked at him dreamily.

"No way. I could stay here for the rest of my life!". And Khaled got wet eyes.

"What is it, my prince?"

"I have to think about our first night. I completely felt in love within a second. And now you're back and this time forever. Please pin me!"

"I don´t have to. It´s reality. Believe it", Angelos said with a grin.

"And how I love your mouth," Khaled added.

"I loved you from the first date on, too. But I did not want to admit it. And I fought against it. Sorry, that's why it took so long. I love you no less than you love me, but you knew that soon! "

"Oh yeah. Your eyes have betrayed you. And Alex has probably seen it, too!"

But the private moment was after a few minutes, because the phone was buzzing.

It was the buzzing before the storm.

It was Nikos, Angelos' friend from the secret service.

"Nice photos, Angelos!"

"Nice? He's an assassin! "

"A naked assassin? ", Nikos thinned.

"What the hell are you talking about?"

"Well, there were fifty nude shots in your file, you, Khaled, you both. And by no means posing, but rather in action! I did not know you from this side! "

Angelos wiped his cell phone. Oh, crap!

"I sent you the wrong file. I'm an idiot!"

"I liked it, something new. And besides, your Khaled has a formidable tool", Nikos teased, who was a confident hetero.

"Very funny. You delete them immediately. I'll send you the right file!"

Then came the sentence that changed everything.

"I think you do not need that. The pictures brought a hit", Nikos said.

A hit? On private pictures of me and Khaled?

"What are you talking about? There's only me and Khaled on it! "

"No. At the end there are three photos, which were probably shot from a roof. In the garden of a neighbor. And his face caused a red light and a 'Bing' in our program", explained Nikos.

Roof photo? Neighbor? Angelos' brain still refused to understand anything.

Oh God! The last photos were those of Alex' infidelity.

"I do not get it. There is a match, but with what?"

The neighbor's photo is 99% consistent with a photo in our archives. And Mr. Neighbor is not a petty criminal. He is a professional killer. Tomas Masaryk, Adam Resniak or ...

"Marco Tardelli", Angelos pressed out.

The hairy fool Alex had slept with.

'The good man is associated with twelve murders. A real professional killer who does not care about ideology. Whoever pays decides!"

"Nikos, I cannot talk anymore. Everything is spinning in my head. I'll call you back!"

"Good. May I keep the photos?"

"If they excite you, gladly!"

Angelos dropped the phone and said to Khaled:

"Please hug me!"

"What's going on?"

"Your assassin is our hairy neighbor!"

"Alex slept with an assassin?"

"You have to arrest him", Khaled said.

"We are not in the Middle East. The picture is not from the crime scene, it shows him after his tete-a-tete with Alex. And sex is not punishable, although in this case I would ... I do not know what evidence Nikos has, but certainly not much, otherwise the hairy killer would have already been arrested.

Besides, it would look like I was arresting the personal rival in revenge. No judge puts a stamp on the arrest warrant under these circumstances!"

"Funny habits", Khaled said.

Angelos smiled.

"Constitutional state. But that's not the point. Resniak or Tardelli probably approached Alex just to be close to the action.

To have a commissioner as a friend means for a criminal: you know everything. When Alex finds out, his self-confidence gets a crack. The guy misused him! "

"But then he's in danger", Khaled interjected. "You have to go to him, immediately!"

Angelos ran to the door but turned back and kissed Khaled.

"You're a good person!"

37

H E IS WHAT? YOU ARE CRAZY. THIS IS ONLY A RISICULOUS BACKLASH ", Alex said.

"Would I act like that? That would be sad", Angelos answered.

Alex sat down at the kitchen table.

"Would you believe Nikos?", Angelos asked.

"It would help me!"

Angelos typed into his cell phone.

"Nikos? Alex wants to ask something. Tell him what you have told me!"

"That Khaled is well equipped?"

Angelos laughed.

"No, you idiot. The rest!"

Alex picked up the phone and listened. You could hear some 'sure?' Or 'quite sure?'

"Thanks, Nikos. I can tell you more tomorrow!", Angelos said.

Silence.

"So, he just chose me because..."

"It looks like that and I'm sorry. It should not damage your ego. You're a good-looking man. Would I have married you otherwise?", Angelos asked.

"It's still humiliating because I felt for it. And ruined everything!"

"Nonsense. It was only a matter of time before we finally would have failed. I really love Khaled and could not resist it anymore!

And: it is like that now. But we must catch him. To confess!"

"We?", Alex asked.

"You and me. And we cannot do it without you! "

"Aha. And what plan do you have in mind?"

"Quite simply, you invite him to dinner, go to bed with him, and then we got him", Angelos said, smiling.

"Should I sleep with a professional killer?"

"Actually, you already did!"

"Touché," Alex said.

"Why wait until after sex?"

"He has to be naked so I can be sure that he has no weapon!"

"You forget his hands!", Alex protested.

"No. You will suggest a bondage game. I remember you like it!"

I hate and love this grin.

Oh yes, I loved it. And I will never ... Stop, Alex!

"And as soon as he will hang on the ropes, you will join us."

Angelos nodded. "But not naked!"

"All right", Alex agreed.

"Good. Then I have one more thing to clarify", Angelos said, reaching for his cell phone. He explained to Khaled what he planned.

"That means Alex would be naked in your presence?"

"So what? Do you think I will get an erection?", Angelos asked.

"I will be there. I will not leave you alone with a professional killer. It may be that he does not want sex. Then you would be in danger!" Angelos considered.

"Perfect. But you leave the interrogation to me. The victim is usually not part if it!"

"Funny rules in Europe", Khaled said.

Angelos laughed.

"And what is bondage, please?" Khaled asked.

"It will be an enjoyable experience for you. But you will need a few lessons before!", Angelos replied.

"I like your lessons", Khaled said.

38

Khaled and Angelos were hiding in the guest room. They had told Alex not to close the bedroom door under any circumstances.

"Say you need fresh air during sex," Angelos suggested.

"Normally, you open the window for that, don´t you?"

"God, then we hang out the door because the carpenter repairs on Monday. Better?"

"Much better. Now, should I cook for a killer?", Alex asked.

"Imagine you're cooking for me", Angelos said.

Silence.

"Sorry, that was nasty!"

"Alright. Everything is a bit difficult for both of us", Alex said.

"For us three", Khaled interposed.

"You are right. Well, a pasta is certainly not wrong with an Italian!"

"Perfect. And Pasta is your specialty", Angelos said.

39

Fudscheirah

Mansoor sat at his desk trying to piece together the puzzle pieces.

How do I get out of that mess? With head.

The killer would have had to get in touch long ago, also because of the money transfer. They wanted to avoid bank transfers. The killer had agreed. Mansoor could not do anything to him because he already knew too much. And is cabled and connected to his agency. Usual reinsurance of the contracting party, who must protect its freelancers.

Maybe Resniak was under pressure and sinking. Certainly, no mistake, if the commissioner was the lover of the victim.

So, calm down, he thought.

Nevertheless, it is strange that there was nothing in the news. Maybe the Greeks have imposed a news blackout. What worried Mansoor: even his contacts on the island couldn´t find out anything. In the hospital he seems to have died, but there was no corpse in the pathology.

The hotel said Nikakis had entrenched himself in his villa - out of grief. Hard to believe that Nikakis is not determined. Hatred would suit him better, according to the general assessment.

Better carry out a double-track strategy, Mansoor thought.

"Your visit arrived", the voice out of his intercom bellowed.

"Royal Highness, welcome!"

"Mansoor, I'm wondering. I always thought you wanted to see me dead. You made a change of heart? "

Because things change, you idiot.

"First of all, let's leave the 'Royal Highness'. We talk on the same level!"

His guest nodded.

"Well, your dad thinks you're a good-for-nothing, a blither, but I see a certain potential. Would you like to become Emir, Raschid? "

40

Alex was visibly restless, which also Resniak registered.

"What about you?", the killer said, who had a special sense.

"Sorry, I just have a hormonal boost!"

Bravo, Alex, Angelos thought.

"I did not know that I had such an effect!", Resniak said.

"Wasn´t that you in the garden shed?"

"Of course. But I had the impression you had a bone to pick with your husband!"

Careful, Alex, Angelos is listening.

"No, it wasn´t that. I just did not think. I did not come because I wanted to sleep with you. It just happened! "

"Do you regret it?", Resniak asked.

"No. Otherwise I would not have invited you today. Would I?"

Alex carried the dishes into the kitchen and put in the Viagra.

I cannot do it, not with him, he thought.

Ten minutes later, they went upstairs and, in fact, Resniak noticed the door.

"Must be repainted. Now take off your clothes!"

Let's get it over, Alex thought. And hopefully I'll be able to bend the knots.

It took exactly 16 minutes.

"Was he so fast with you?", Khaled asked softly.

"No. But it was me who laid next to him",
Angelos answered.

Khaled had to put his hand over his mouth to
avoid laughing.

Suddenly Alex stood in the room, of course
naked.

"He's packed", he said and went back.

"Bend me off", Resniak roared.

Angelos and Khaled entered the room.

"Jassas, Mr. Tardelli. Or Resniak or whatever!"

'That was a nasty trick," Resniak said.

"Not nastier than murder", Angelos answered
succinctly.

"Good, Alex. Will you please go to the cellar?
I need the soldering iron and the extension
cable with switch. And finally get dressed!"

Khaled glanced at Angelos.

"I have no erection, if that's what you mean!"

"I'm very happy about that", Khaled
answered.

When Alex came back with the soldering
iron, Resniak visibly became nervous and
pulled the knitting.

"Alex! Khaled! Raise his legs up", Angelos said.

A minute later Resniak had the soldering iron
in the rectum.

"Now we're doing a little functional test",
Angelos said with a grin.

"NOOOOO!"

"Yes." And Angelos pressed the switch.

Resniak started to sweat heavily. Then his
body twitched, and he screamed.

Angelos broke the connection.

"Interesting. That's what we at home as well"
Khaled said, who had a personal grudge,
because Resniak wanted to kill him.

"In Greece that is forbidden. Of course, not
valid for the Emir of Mikonos", Alex said.

"As if you had always taken care of the rules",
Angelos growled.

"Should not we interrogate the gentleman?"
Khaled suggested.

"You are right, my prince. So, we know you
are a professional killer. And always
remember the soldering iron when
answering!"

"Yes. I am. What do you want?"

"What was your assignment? And who gave
the order? "

"My job? I had two! "

Angelos looked startled.

"Why two?"

"The archaeologist and the prince!"

"The explosion was you? What have the two
cases to do with each other? "

"Nothing, Heavens. It was two separate
orders!"

"Ok. Of course, we would like to know who
has placed the orders. For motivation, I press
the switch again", Angelos said.

"NOOOOO!"

"The guy from Delos had embezzled valuable
coins instead of handing them over to his
trader. Some Romanians!"

"Don´t you know more?"

"No?"

Khaled said to Angelos, "Push it!"
Resniak screamed.
"It smells like meat", Angelos said.
"Grilled meet", Alex added.
"Please, please! I say everything. It's not that a killer does not know his clients. The self-destructing CDs are a TV fairy tale. We need accurate data. Habits, timelines and other things. We have no way – and no time - to get this information alone. We work alone. For reinsurance we, including the agency, require an explanation for the order and the name of the client.
Safe for the client. We receive all documents on paper by courier. No CD, no email. Nice old-fashioned, but the safest method. Afterwards everything gets burned. I already burned the stuff about the archaeologist. That's why I do not remember anything except that it was a Romanian name! Believe me! No! Wait!
Would you like to have something to drink? Alex, please "
Alex looked questioningly at Angelos.
"He's your friend", Angelos said.
Alex went down to the kitchen.
'That was not nice", Khaled said softly.
Angelos breathed.
"You criticize me. Well, finally. And you are right. That was wrong!"
When Alex came with a cup of water, Angelos said:
"Sorry, that saying was silly!"

"It´s ok".

"Enough water. Now to the assassination",
Angelos said.

"The order came from my agency and was to
neutralize the Crown Prince. And the fee was
generous. My highest ever!"

"That was only appropriate", Angelos said,
smiling at Khaled.

"A precision shot did not work. No quiet
place. The bodyguards told Fudscheirah that
the target would be at 2.30 pm at the port to
take over his yacht. "

"The target? I am a human. Come on
Angelos, give me the switch", Khaled said.
"NOOOO, please!"

After a short break Resniak continued:

"In the harbor, only a frontal attack was
realizable, from the car or the motorcycle.
With the motorcycle I can escape better and
do not get stuck in the heavy traffic. I could
not foresee the problem with the trucks. In
addition: that you are so strong motorized. A
serious mistake!"

"Yes, the SUV was a good idea!"

Angelos grinned at Alex.

"Further. Let's get to the client, money transfer
and so on! "

"I got some documents. By courier. The
papers must have come from the highest
level in the Emirates. A private security
company was named. But my agency knew
that this is just a fake of the local intelligence
agency!"

"Mansoor, the miserable bastard", Khaled shouted.

"And gay too!"

Angelos and Alex turned their heads towards Khaled at the same time.

"Do not ask, Angelos! Because I cannot lie!" And Angelos did not.

"But for sure on behalf of your father. Well, how did the money transfer work?"

"Not at all. I should fly to Fudscheirah and pick up the money in person! "

"But that's too dangerous, ain´t it? The client gets rid of the witness, in his own country ", Alex said.

"Not at all. We reassure ourselves before. With the little button on the lapel I'm in constant contact with the agency. The handover gets filmed and the meeting point is determined by us. We are not tired of life. I just didn´t do it yet because I was not sure if ... "

".. the target is dead at all", Angelos added.

"Okay, then we should leave it uncertain. You fly there to get your money!"

The "WHAAT?" came from Khaled and Alex at the same time.

Even Resniak understood nothing.

"You let me go?", he asked. But there is something in the wind, he thought.

"What are you doing, Angelos?", Khaled asked.

'That's easy. You're going down to the kitchen with Alex and you're having one or two espresso´s!"

"No. Do not leave me alone with this madman!", Resniak shouted.

"Do not worry", Angelos said, pulling the cable out of the socket. "Satisfied?"

Resniak breathed a sigh of relief.

"And you two: downstairs!"

Khaled and Alex understood nothing but followed the instruction.

When they were outside, Angelos sat down on the edge of the bed.

"So, Mr. Resniak or Tardelli. I'll let you go. The condition is that you will bowl down something for me. I thought of ... "

Five minutes later, a dressed Resniak left the house and marched to his home.

Angelos, however, came into the kitchen and looked into two questioning faces.

"I'll explain it to you in a few days!"

"Okay", Khaled said.

"Ok?", Alex asked. "You are even more obedient than me!"

"No, Alex, I´m in love. I trust him without doubts", Khaled replied.

"Besides, I would like to do such a bondage game later. But I still have a question!"

"Which would be, my prince?"

"The soldering iron is hopefully not part of the game?"

And Angelos got a laugh attack.

"Do not worry. Only MY soldering iron will be used!"

41

The Emir was sitting at his desk holding the oxygen mask in his hands. It was getting worse; the pain was also increasing.

Still no word as to whether Khaled had been eliminated.

If Mansoor screwed that up, I'll send him to the desert, but in the truest sense of the word.

Three men entered the room.

"Mansoor! Raschid! What are you doing here? And who is the third? And anyway: you do not march into the Emir´s office without signing up!"

Raschid smiled.

"Should I have made an appointment with myself?"

The Emir was too ill to grasp the meaning of the sentence immediately.

"What do you want? Is Khaled dead? I expect an explanation, Mansoor!"

"There was a small change of plan!"

"Only I make changes. Who do you think you are?", the Emir exclaimed during a coughing fit.

"Take care, Highness", Mansoor said.

"Why do you say 'Highness' to him? That's my address", Raschid said.

Even before the Emir understood, Resniak stood behind the Emir, grabbed his head and tore it to the right. Even before the oxygen mask hit the ground, the Emir was already in the empire of the seventy virgins.

42

C an I ask you something, sweetie?", Khaled asked.
The two were in bed and cuddled.
"Sure. You can ask me anything", Angelos said.
"What did you negotiate with the killer?"
"Now I can tell you, because it's over. Do you really want to know all the details?"
"Absolutely!"
"I had a conversation with Mr. Mansoor afterwards", Angelos said.
Khaled looked surprised.
"You talked to my killer?"
Angelos laughed.
"You are not dead, and he was just the executive arm. However, I called him. I recorded the conversation. Do you want to hear it?"

Khaled nodded.

He heard the following:

"Angelos Nikakis here. You know who I am. Khaled lives and that becomes a problem for you. The Emir will dismiss you at best, if not more. I have a solution to offer. Your killer is now my killer. He will come to Fudscheirah and you will give him a chance to meet the Emir. There he will do what he is trained to do. That would be the best outcome you can hope for because it is the only way you would be out of danger. Maybe you already have one of the two other sons of the Emir as successor. You should prepare him to wear the crown a little earlier. Of course, you must consider everything. I'll call again in an hour! "

Khaled put the phone aside.

"And he has …?"

"Of course, he has. Your Emirate has a new Emir, for two hours ago. What's your drunken brother's name?"

"Raschid!"

"Long live Emir Raschid!" Angelos said.

"I have a genius in my bed", Khaled said.

"Do not exaggerate, but: anyone who wants to do something to you, will pay for it! And Messrs. Raschid and Mansoor had to promise to leave you alone. That was the deal.

We have our peace, because Resniak has recorded everything and I have the recorded conversation.

Khaled looked at Angelos with bright eyes that emit tears.
I have arrived, he thought.

43

The Prime minister", Khaled said, handing Angelos the phone.
"A call from you does not bode well!" Migiakis laughed.
"Already looked in the internet? Your father-in-law has died. Not quite voluntarily it says!"
"My grief is limited", Angelos said calmly.
"I am sure it is. My secret service is chirping to me that they have found a professional killer on Mikonos, informed you and he was able to escape. That does not sound like you", Migiakis said sarcastically.
"Rumors say that the same killer is not entirely innocent of the death of the Emir, I mean the right one. Not you."
"What do I know about some coup in an Emirate thousands of miles away?", Angelos said.

"Never say again, I would use unfair practices", Migiakis replied.

Angelos laughed.

"How is the relation to your mother-in-law?" Migiakis growled.

"You're welcome to use my contacts if you want"´, a cheerful Angelos said.

'Thanks for the offer. I would only ask you not to move any other heads of state to the afterlife. Dates with their ambassadors are sometimes uncomfortable!"

"I promise", Angelos said.

"Uh, by the way: I'm not the number two on your list?", Migiakis asked.

Angelos laughed.

"I am treating you with the greatest benevolence! If my applications for funding continue to be approved!"

Migiakis laughed.

"Blackmailer. And we will talk about my mother-in-law! "

Volume 4: "Spy"
will be released in
February!

Already published in GERMAN and GREEK:

Paul Katsitis – Royals

Zehn Seemeilen entfernt von Mykonos wird ein großes Gasfeld entdeckt. Bürgermeister und Kommissar Angelos Nikakis greift zu allen (auch illegalen) Tricks, um Bohrtürme in der Ägäis zu verhindern.

Als dann eine Prinzessin des Emirats Katar während eines Besuchs auf Mykonos entführt wird, scheint es zunächst nicht so, als würde ein Zusammenhang bestehen. Wenige Tage später ist die Prinzessin tot – und Angelos Nikakis sitzt im Gefängnis.

Paul Katsitis - Trauma

Chefermittler und Bürgermeister Angelos Nikakis glaubt es zunächst nicht: auf der trockenen Insel Mykonos soll ein Golfplatz errichtet werden. Als Nikakis den Investor trifft, glaubt er ihn zu kennen. Bevor er sich erinnert, ereignen sich zwei Morde.
Angelos´ Ehemann Alex findet währenddessen heraus, woher Angelos den Investor kennt.
Bald geschieht ein dritter Mord. Und der Täter ist Alex.

Paul Katsitis – Der Putsch

1967 putscht in Griechenland das Militär. Hellas und auch Mykonos ächzen unter der Diktatur.
52 Jahre später gibt es wieder einen Regierungswechsel in Athen. Doch die Ereignisse von damals werfen ihre späten Schatten.
Ein Flugzeugabsturz und Kommissar Angelos Nikakis sorgen dafür, dass es zu einem politischen Erdbeben kommt.

Paul Katsitis – Glut

Der Alptraum aller Chora-Bewohner wird wahr. Ein Großbrand wütet in den engen Gassen der Stadt. Eine knifflige Aufgabe nicht nur für die Feuerwehr, sondern auch für Kommissar und Bürgermeister Angelos Nikakis. Denn in einem Haus findet man eine Leiche. Ein Brandopfer, denken viele. Doch sie wurde erschossen. Drei weitere Morde und der Wiederaufbau lassen Angelos kaum Zeit Luft zu holen.

Paul Katsitis - Abseits

Im Stadion von Mykonos wird die Leiche eines Mannes gefunden. Da der Mann Fan von Olympiakos Piräus war, geraten alle Anhänger des Konkurrenzvereins Panathinaikos Athen in Verdacht. Die Indizien lassen zunächst keine andere These zu und der Hass zwischen beiden Lagern ist tatsächlich so groß, dass auch ein Mord im Bereich des Möglichen liegt.
Doch als Kommissar Angelos Nikakis in die Welt der Spielerscouts eintaucht, stellt er fest, dass es um ganz andere Dinge ging: um Menschen-handel, Pädophilie und natürlich eine Menge Geld!

Paul Katsitis – Die Maske

ohne Vorwarnung in den Rücken geschossen hat, steht er bald unter Anklage.
Im Schatten des Prozesses gelingt es einem neuen, besonders brutalen Drogenhändler, genannt „Máská", sein Netzwerk auszubauen. Und er zögert auch nicht, als sich ihm die Gelegenheit bietet, Kommissar a.D. Angelos Nikakis aus dem Weg zu räumen.

Paul Katsitis – Die Bestie von Mykonos

Zwei Kriminalbeamte, Alexandros und Angelos, quittieren den Dienst und eröffnen gemeinsam auf Mykonos eine Bar. Nebenher betreiben sie eine kleine Privat-Detektei. Da die Polizei chronisch unterbesetzt ist, werden Alex und Angelos – wegen ihrer Erfahrung - regelmäßig hinzugezogen.
Mykonos ist in Aufruhr. Offensichtlich foltert, vergewaltigt und tötet ein Mann junge Touristen. Um ihn zu stellen, bleibt nichts anderes übrig, als dass Angelos den Lockvogel spielt – mit furchtbaren Konsequenzen ...

Paul Katsitis – Rache

Im Kloster Ano Mera auf Mykonos wird ein Priester tot aufgefunden, dessen Leiche übel zugerichtet ist. Es sieht nach einem Rachemord aus – doch wofür?

Paul Katsitis - Hass

Es ist ein besonderer Fall für die beiden Ermittler Alex und Angelos Nikakis. Die Leiche eines jungen Mannes wird in den Dünen gefunden. Am und im Körper des Toten findet sich die DNA von Angelos.
Er wird verhaftet.

Paul Katsitis – Inzest

Ein Bräutigam, der sich am Tag der Hochzeit vom Balkon stürzt und eine Mädchenleiche in einer Wagenpresse. Zwei Fälle für die beiden Ex-Kommissare Alex und Angelos Nikakis Zwei Fälle, die sich nach und nach aufeinander zu bewegen.

Paul Katsitis – Der-Drei-Sterne-Mord

Im besten Restaurant der Insel wird der Chefkoch, ehemals Leibkoch Gaddafis, mit durchschnittener Kehle aufgefunden. Ein schwieriger Fall für Alex und Angelos, zumal die eigene Familie mit beteiligt ist. Der Fall erfährt eine erstaunliche Wendung, als die beiden Ermittler erfahren, dass der britische Außenminister Mykonos besucht – auf dem Landsitz des griechischen Premierministers.

Paul Katsitis - Tattoo

Zwei Highlights stehen auf dem Programm des Wochenendes: ein hochdotiertes Beachvolleyball-Turnier und die Eröffnung der ersten Spielbank auf der Insel.
Nicht ins „Event-Wochenende" passen zwei Tote: ein 19-jähriger Junge und einer der Beachvolleyballspieler. An dessen „natürlichem Tod" haben die Ermittler Alex und Angelos so ihre Zweifel.

Paul Katsitis – Skalpell

Am Strand von Ornos wird eine Frauenleiche gefunden. Es ist die Tochter des Bürgermeisters. Der Leiche fehlen Nieren und Leber.

Doch es geht bei der Mordserie nicht nur um Organe, wie die beiden Ermittler Alexandros und Angelos Nikakis bald feststellen. Es existiert ein komplexes Netzwerk, das verschiedene kriminelle Felder abdeckt, und so mancher Inselbewohner ist darin verstrickt.

Hints

EYP is the Greek secret service.
ERT ist the Greek state TV.